WASHOE COUNTY LIBRARY
3 1235 03504 4317

D1016707

VIZ GRAPHIC NOVEL

RANMA 1/2™

13

This volume contains
RANMA 1/2 PART SEVEN #3 (second half) through
#9 (first half) in their entirety.

Story & Art by Rumiko Takahashi

English Adaptation by Gerard Jones & Toshifumi Yoshida

*

Touch-Up Art & Lettering/Wayne Truman
Cover Design/Hidemi Sahara
Editor/Trish Ledoux
Assistant Editor/Bill Flanagan

*

Managing Editor/Hyoe Narita
Editor-in-Chief/Satoru Fujii
Publisher/Seiji Horibuchi

*

First published by Shogakukan, Inc. in Japan

*

For the purposes of publication in English,
the artwork in this publication
is in reverse from the original Japanese version.

Printed in Canada

*

Published by Viz Communications, Inc.
P.O. Box 77010
San Francisco, CA 94107

*

10 9 8 7 6 5 4 3 2 1
First printing, March 1999

Vizit us at our World Wide Web site at www.viz.com,
our Internet magazine, j-pop.com, at www.j-pop.com,
and Animerica at www.animerica-mag.com

VIZ GRAPHIC NOVEL

RANMA 1/2™

STORY & ART BY

RUMIKO TAKAHASHI

CONTENTS

PART 1
THE MARK OF THE GODS

WHERE AM I NOW...?
SWIP
RRRSHLL
HM?
ZHA
FOOD!
SHK

DONK
BWAK
GONK

FUMP

FEH,
TRYING TO ATTACK ME...?
WHAT A FOOL-HARDY GUY.
SQOOSH

HUH?
GWI

IT'S JUST A WITHERED OLD MAN...
FOOD..

KIMEN SCHOOL OF MARTIAL ARTS CALLIGRAPHY?
BWACH BWACH
RAMEN
CUP O' SQUID
CUP NOODLE

I AM A WELL KNOWN AND RESPECTED MARTIAL ARTS CALLIGRAPHER.
...NONE OTHER.
SHLUP SHLOP
SSSHHHHLLLORRPP
SUPER NOODLE
AND WHAT EXACTLY *IS* MARTIAL ARTS CALLIGRAPHY?

WHEW...
CHK CHK
POM POM

NOW THEN...
FFFWIP

WHAT ARE YOU DOING ?
MOOSH...

IN RETURN FOR YOUR FOOD, I WAS GOING TO BESTOW UPON YOU MY MARTIAL ARTS CALLIGRAPHY.

A PERSON'S POWER COMES FROM THE HYPO-GASTRIC REGION...
...BASICALLY, THE ABDOMEN.
Hypogastrium Region
ESPECIALLY IN MARTIAL ARTS, IT'S IMPORTANT TO CONCENTRATE YOUR *CHI* IN YOUR ABDOMEN.

MARTIAL ARTS CALLIGRAPHY IS A TECHNIQUE WHICH, WHEN USED TO MARK A PERSON'S ABDOMEN WITH A SPECIAL SYMBOL...
SHWAA...
...THAT PERSON CAN DRAW UPON INCREDIBLE STRENGTH...

SO IT'S A KIND OF CHARM?
GRRIK GRRIK
STICK O' INK

DON'T YOU WANT TO BE THE STRONGEST MAN IN THE WORLD!?

WHERE ARE YOU GOING?
FEH, HOW LAME...
SHF

STRONGEST IN THE WORLD...?
TWITCH

NOW EXPOSE YOUR ABDOMEN!
YOU'VE GOT NOTHING TO LOSE!
DM DM DM DM DM DM
...THAT I COULD DEFEAT RANMA!?
"STRONGEST IN THE WORLD" WOULD MEAN...

THE KIMEN SCHOOL OF MARTIAL ARTS CALLIGRAPHY ULTIMATE TECHNIQUE...!
FWA
FWA
THE MARK OF THE BATTLING GOD!
SHA!

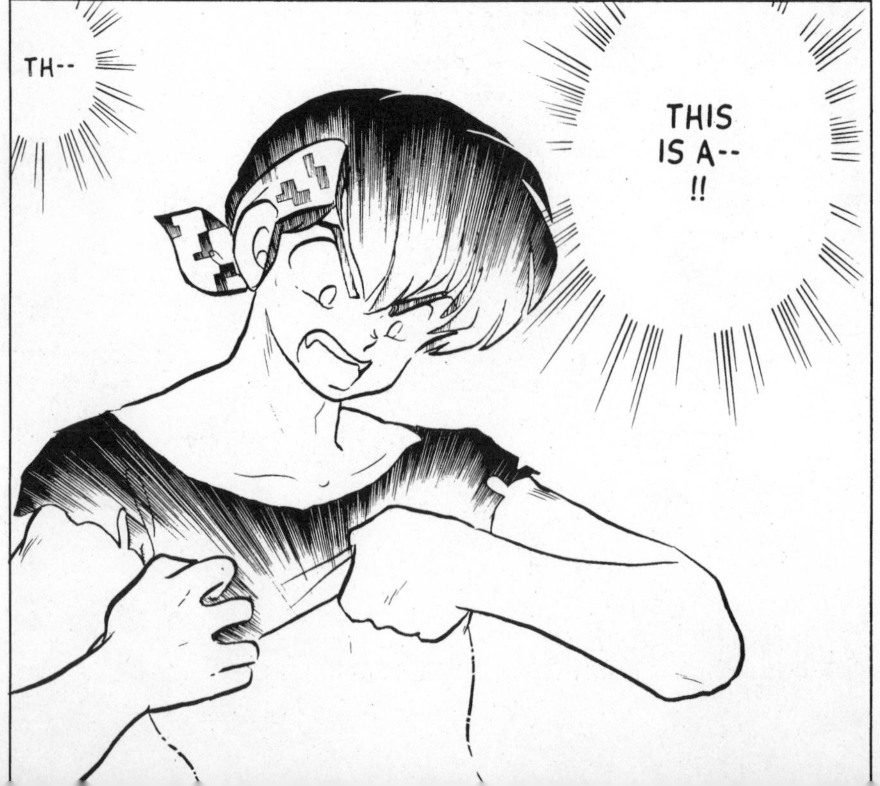

THIS IS A-- !!
TH--

RYOGA, YOU JERK...!
CHIIIIIIRRUP
CHIIII CHIIII
HE CHALLENGES ME TO A FIGHT...
AIRMAIL
Ranma,
Come to the vacant lot in the third district tomorrow at noon.
—Ryoga Hibiki
HE'S A WEEK LATE NOW... NO SENSE OF DIRECTION AT ALL.
GETS LOST IN HIS OWN YARD.
HHSSHH
MYŌSHINKAN
DŌKAN
YŌKAN
DOJO
SHF
SHF
WHERE'S THE VACANT LOT?
SHF
SHF
HEY...
YOU JUST WALKED BY IT.

OKAY... THEN.
WHAT'S WITH ALL THOSE DOJO SIGNS?
FLOMP
ALONG THE WAY...
I CHALLENGED A FEW DOJOS...

WHOA...
I GUESS YOU MUST HAVE GOTTEN A BIT BETTER.

COME AT ME ANY WAY YOU LIKE, RANMA...
PRETTY CONFIDENT, AREN'TCHA?
OKAY THEN, HERE I COME!
TAH!
LET'S SEE WHAT YOU'VE GOT!

sSS

TAP
HUH?

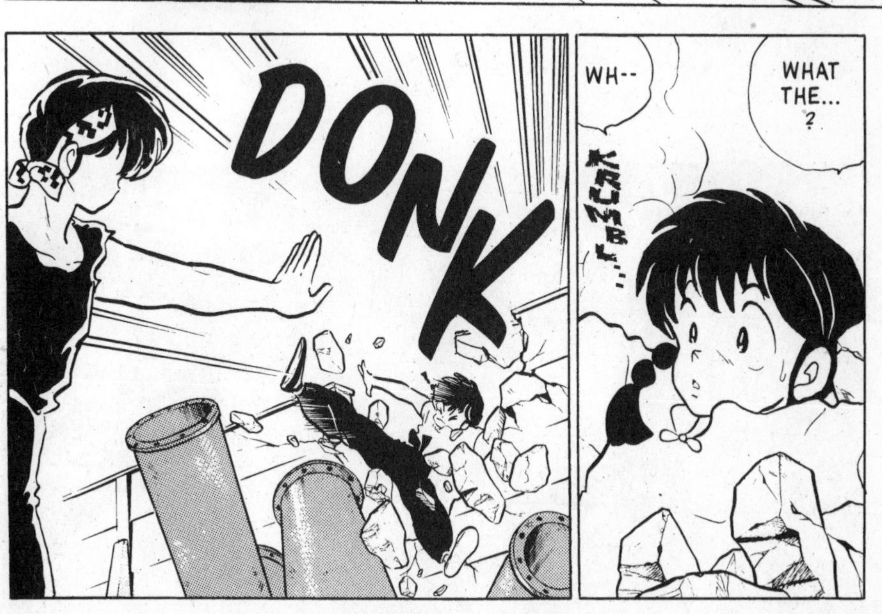
WHAT THE...?
WH--
KRUMBL...
DONK

WHAT'S THE MATTER, RANMA?
IF YOU DON'T COME AT ME SERIOUSLY, YOU'LL GET HURT.
YOU DON'T HAVE TO TELL ME TWICE...

HERE I COME!
SHP
VWIP

FLIP
FLIP
FLIP
NGH!
NGH!

HE'S READING MY MOVES!
IMPOSSIBLE!

SHP
TAP

DWOOOOM
NNNGH!

I BEAT HIM...
...WITH ONLY MY PINKIE...

.....
I'VE GOT NO USE FOR YOU NOW.
FARE-WELL, RANMA.
DMF

...YOU COULD BE THE ONE WHO COULD BEAT ME.
I THOUGHT IF ANYONE...
SIGH...
RYOGA...?

...MARTIAL ARTS CALLI-GRAPHY?
UH-HUH.
WITH THE MARK OF THE BATTLING GOD UPON YOUR ABDOMEN, YOU'LL BECOME THE MOST POWERFUL MAN IN THE WORLD!
SHA!
AND WITH THE MARKINGS...
I *DID* BECOME THE STRONGEST MAN IN THE WORLD...
BUT AT THE SAME TIME...

...I'VE ALSO BECOME THE *MOST TRAGIC* MAN, AS WELL!
FWUP!

HHSSHH
DOJO

SHFF

SCRUB
SCRUB
SCRUB
SCRUB
SCRUB
SCRUB

IT'S USE-LESS...
...IT'S NOT SOMETHING YOU CAN JUST RUB OFF.
sigh

ffp

SCOUR SCOUR
SCOUR
SCOUR
SCOUR

THAT HURTS!
BWAK

I TRIED TO GET IT OFF MYSELF...
HHSSHH
...I TRIED PRACTICALLY EVERYTHING...

BUT...
HEY, OLD MAN!
GET THIS DOODLE OFF OF ME!
NOW!
THERE'S ONLY ONE WAY TO GET IT OFF.

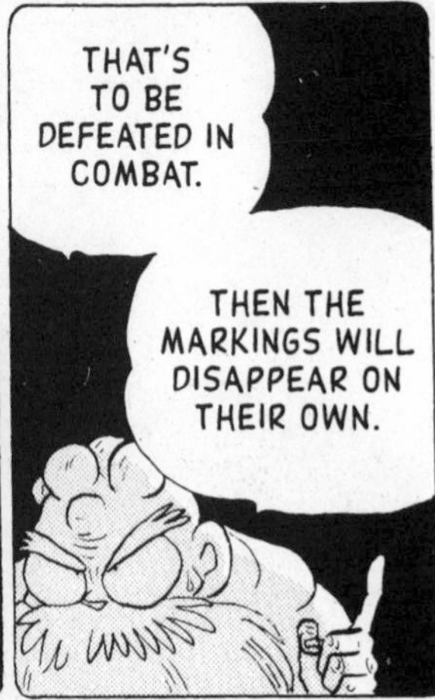
THAT'S TO BE DEFEATED IN COMBAT.
THEN THE MARKINGS WILL DISAPPEAR ON THEIR OWN.

I SEE...
SO *THAT'S* WHY YOU'VE BEEN CHALLENGING ALL THESE DOJOS...
OF COURSE, I WON EVERY TIME...

LOOKS TO ME LIKE...

I'VE REACHED A LEVEL OF GREATNESS IN MY MARTIAL ARTS THAT YOU COULD NEVER HOPE TO ACHIEVE, RANMA.

FARE-WELL!
STOMP
--WAIT!

THAT MARKING...
I'LL GET RID OF IT FOR YOU!

LIKE I'VE TOLD YOU...
THE ONLY WAY FOR ME TO LOSE IT IS IN COMBAT.

SO, WHAT I'M TELLING YOU IS THAT I'LL BEAT YOU SOMEHOW!
.....

RYOGA...
YOU'RE THE...
...ONLY MAN THAT I CONSIDER TO BE MY RIVAL.

!

AND YOU CAME TO ME, BECAUSE YOU NEEDED MY HELP, RIGHT!?

ALL RIGHT !?
LEAVE IT TO ME!
SIIIIGH
RANMA...
YOU'RE...

SUCH A NICE GUY!
BWAK

HHSSHHHH
HM ?

AFTER ALL THAT TALK...
HE RUNS AWAY!
I'LL...BEAT HIM...YOU... JUST... WATCH...!

RANMA...!

PART 2
FACE OFF!

天道道場
ALL RIGHT, RANMA. COME AT ME!
twee twee twee
RYOGA... WHAT IN THE HELL...?
SHUT UP!
I HAVE TO LOSE TO YOU, REMEMBER?!

AND YOU DON'T THINK I CAN BEAT YOU...
HUH.

UNTIL I LOSE A FIGHT...
...I'LL NEVER BE ABLE TO RUB AWAY...
...THE FACE OF THE BATTLING GOD!

I'LL SHOW *YOU* WHAT --
...UNLESS YOU'RE HANDICAPPED ?!
DSH

RRRRRRGH...
...WELL, RANMA !?
I *SAID,* COME *AT* ME!
TWIK TWIK

RYEW
SMUNCH
DONK

JIIIIINNN
chirrup chirrup chirrup

TM TM TM TM TM TM TM TM
FWAFWA FWA

O-KAY!
THE SCROLL OF SECRET BLOWS!
FWA

CURSE YOU, RANMA.
IF I CAN'T COUNT ON *YOU*, WHO CAN I?
sigh

HYAA!
THE SAOTOME DESPERATION STRIKE!!
REALLY ?!
I'M NOT THE SAME OPPONENT I WAS A MINUTE AGO!
HEH HEH HEH! PREPARE YOURSELF!
ta!

EH ?
RYOGA !

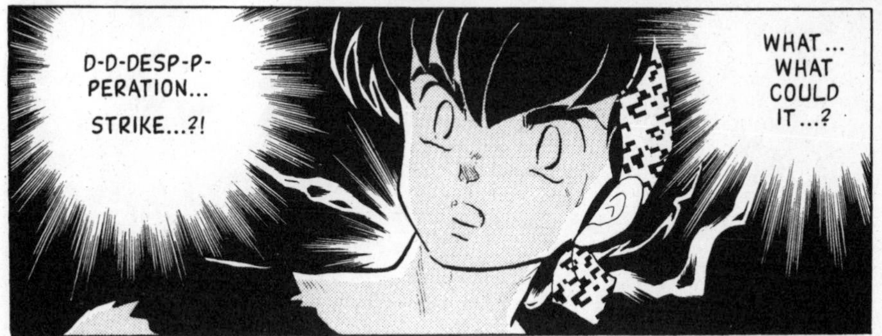
WHAT... WHAT COULD IT...?
D-D-DESP-P-PERATION... STRIKE...?!

HEY
!
WHAT'S
THAT
!?
FWIP
HUH
?

hsSh
HE FELL
FOR IT!

FOX-
FU!!
THE SECRET
OF ATTACKING
FROM BEHIND
LIKE A HUNTING
CANINE!
SHA!
KLONG
SHKK
.....
TWIK
TWIK

OKAY...SAOTOME DESPERATION STRIKE #2!
FWA

STRIKING AN ENEMY TO THE GROUND WITH A SINGLE BLOW, LIKE A TIGER!
FELINE-FU!!

WHAT IDIOT WOULD FALL FOR THAT?!
GOOOSH
Oh! The old D.S.#2!

LOOK! A HUNDRED YEN!

WHERE ?!
WHERE ?!
SHOOOOMM

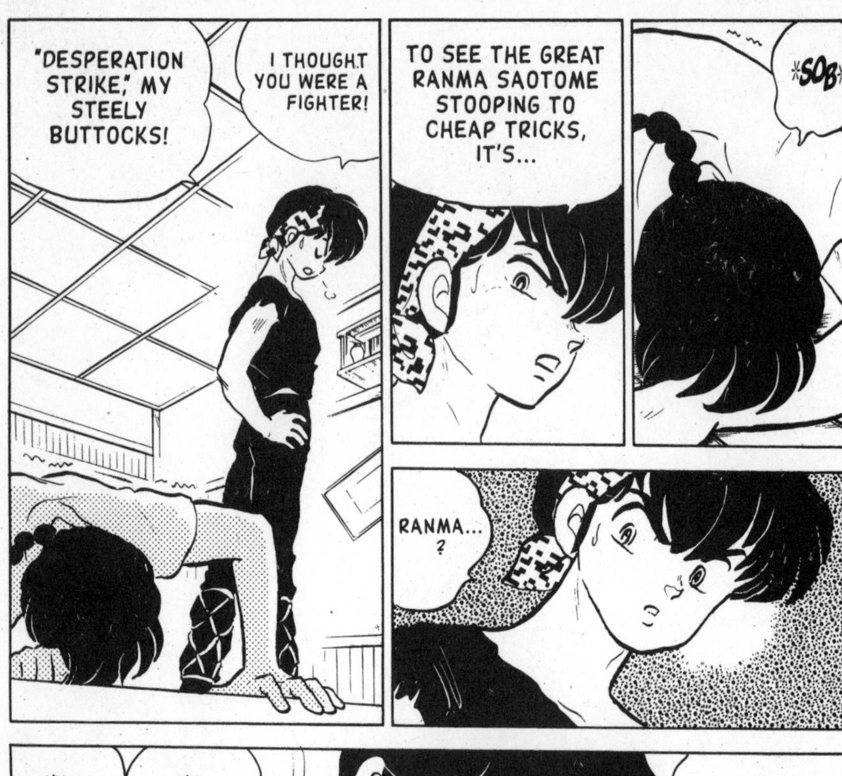
"DESPERATION STRIKE," MY STEELY BUTTOCKS!
I THOUGHT YOU WERE A FIGHTER!
TO SEE THE GREAT RANMA SAOTOME STOOPING TO CHEAP TRICKS, IT'S...
SOB
RANMA...?

I'M... I'M SORRY RYOGA...
I'M JUST SO WEAK...
I CAN'T... S-S-SAVE YOU FROM YOUR CURSE...

I'M SO... SO... SORRRR-RRRRRY...!
BOO HOO HOO HOO
N-N-NO...! RANMA...

PWINK

I'VE JUST BECOME...
...TOO *GOOD* FOR YOU!
sigh

IT'S NOT YOUR FAULT.
DON'T BE SO HARD ON YOURSELF.

SSSHHHH

...LULLING THE ENEMY INTO DROPPING HIS GUARD LIKE A TOAD IN THE ROAD!
FLAT-FROG-FU!!

THE *ULTIMATE* SAOTOME DESPERATION STRIKE...
WA-HA-HA! YOU FELL FOR IT!
B-KEEE!
BONK

AND THE DAY WILL NEVER DAWN WHEN I...
hhsSh
...CAN'T BEAT A PIG!
RRRR
AAAAAH!
DWOOOM
sigh...
P-CHAN!
hyoi

WHAT AWFUL PERSON...

WHAT HAPPENED TO YOU?! WHO DREW THIS?!
B-KEEE

...WOULD DOODLE SOMETHING...
...TO MAKE A POOR LITTLE PIG LOOK *STUPID?!*
STAB STAB

SIGH

P-CHAN, WAIT!
KWEE KWEEE

MY AKANE... *SAW* IT...!
SHE SAW IT...

...LOOK *STUPID*... !!
...LOOK STUPID...
NOOOOOOOOOOO

POOR IDIOT...

HEY, C'MON, MAN...

LISTEN...
I BEEN THINKIN'...

THAT DOODLE OF YOURS...IT'S NOT AS HOPELESS AS YOU THINK...

WHAT...?

HE KNOWS A WAY TO GET RID OF IT...HE'S ABOUT TO TELL ME...
FWA

WELCOME, New Employees!
BWA HA HA HA HA HA

...THINKING?!
BOOM
YOU'RE A FUNNY GUY, RYOGA! I'M GLAD I HIRED YOU!
HOO HOO HA HA
GET A LOAD O' THIS!!
HEY, EVERY-BODY!
tee-hee!
he's so funny!
IS THAT...WHAT YOU CALL...
IT COULD BE GREAT AT PARTIES, Y'KNOW?

P-CHAN, WHERE ARE YOU?!
LET ME WASH THAT STUPID DOODLE OFF!
HM ?
dok
WHONK
POOM!
BECAUSE OF YOU... YOU...
...AKANE SAW THE MARK ON P-CHAN'S PIGGY TUMMY!
GRRN GRRN GRRN
MEANING I'LL NEVER...
...EVER BE ABLE...
Sobb!

SO
TELL
ME
WHY...
OH
RIGHT.
VSH
...TO LET
HER SEE MY
STOMACH!

RYOGA...
?
...SHE'D WANT
TO SEE YOUR
STUPID
STOMACH,
ANYWAY!?
VWOP

...KANE...
?
A...

THE SAME DOODLE AS P-CHAN...?

SHK SHK SHK SHK SHK SHK
KROOOM

WHAT'S GOING ON HERE...?
YOU... Y-Y-YOU...
THERE, THAT WASN'T SO BAD, WAS IT...?
EH-HEH-HEH-HEH

PART 3
THE MARK OF THE PIG

OWOOO
BOW
BOW
BOW

NO. I'M POSITIVE...

THE DOODLE ON P-CHAN...
...AND THE ONE ON RYOGA...
...WERE THE SAME...

BUT WHY?!
OHHHH, RANMA...
fwip
WHY DO YOU KEEP TURNING AWAY FROM ME?
LOOK IN A MIRROR.
GWREE

THERE'S SOMETHING ABOUT P-CHAN...AND RYOGA...
fwip

...WHAT ARE YOU HIDING FROM ME?
GWREE
D-DON'T BE STUPID.
NO... PLEASE, NO...
DON'T LET HER FIGURE IT OUT...
B-BMP B-BMP B-BMP B-BMP
HE HAS TO BE...
SHH

HE HAS
TO BE *ONE*
AND THE
SAME!
BRRRRRR

THE SAME
PERSON DREW
ON RYOGA
AND P-CHAN!

.....
.....

AND...
--WHOA.
HOLD
IT.
I WON'T
LET YOU
SAY IT.

I MUST
CONFESS!
SHWOP

WAY TO GO, SAOTOME !
WAY TO GO...
IT WAS ME!
ME...AND ME ALONE!
FWA

HOW DID I GET TO BE SO GOOD?
I CAN'T BELIEVE I'M DOING THIS FOR THAT MORON...
heh

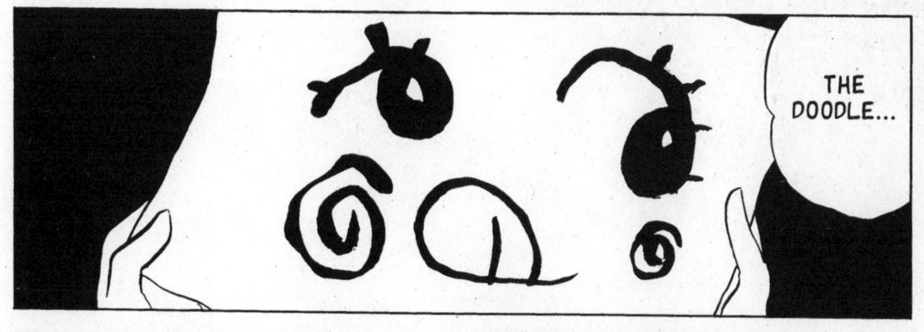
THE DOODLE...

YOU FOOL !
BWOK
...WASN'T DRAWN THIS BADLY!

RYOGA... ?
DEAREST AKANE...

AS LONG AS I HAVE THIS FACE ON MY BELLY...
...MY TERRIBLE SECRET MAY BE EXPOSED...

...I BID YOU...FARE-WELL.

HUH... ?
YOU WHAT ?

RYOGA ?!
I LEAVE ON A QUEST !
SPOING

RANMA!
YOU ARE HIDING SOMETHING !

WHAT IS GOING ON HERE...?!

RANMA...?

...CRYING, NO LESS.
DOLT.
FARE-WELL...
WHAT A MAROON...

STILL...I CAN'T JUST LET HIM SUFFER...

I'VE GOT TO FIND A WAY TO *BEAT* THE POOR DOPE...
BUT RIGHT NOW, HE'S THE BEST FIGHTER THERE IS...

EVEN DESPERATION STRIKES ARE USELESS...
THERE'S NO OPENING TO...

--OPENING ?!
THAT'S *IT!*

I'VE STILL GOT ONE CHANCE!
sha

tweee
twee

hff
hfff
hffff
shmp
shmp

SO...
TIRED...
WALKED ALL NIGHT...BUT COULDN'T REST...
...KNOWING I'LL NEVER SEE MY AKANE AGAIN...
One-two! One-two!
.....
...Ryoga. How's it goin'.

I'VE WALKED BACK TO WHERE I ST-
gasp
IT.... IT CAN'T BE!

RRRRRRRR
OH, PLEASE CATCH MY BALL FOR ME!
PYONG
EH ?

HWA
WHAT -- ?!
AN OPENING !

BWIK
YES! I LANDED A...

POOOOM
...BLOW ?

WHO...
WHAT...
?
Huh..?
GNSH

M-MISS, ARE YOU...
?
I WAS ONLY PL-PLAYING VOLLEYBALL... YOU DIDN'T HAVE T-TO HIT ME...!

I'M... I'M SORRY.
WHEN ANYONE CHARGES ME, MY BODY JUST REACTS.

PLEASE FORGIVE ME.
HEH HEH HEH... THIS TIME HE'S WIDE OPEN...
SMIRK
BOW
boing

ELBOW...
HYAAA

...JAB
?
BWOK

GYAAAH!
I HIT A HELP-LESS LITTLE GIRL...TWICE!
HWRRRRR

HEY!
WHERE'D YOU GO?!

BLOOSH

IT'S STRANGE...
BUT WHAT DOES IT MEAN...?
TM TM TM
CLINIC
Reasonable Rates

WHEN RYOGA LEFT...
P-CHAN DISAPPEARED TOO...

CAN IT BE...?
NO... NO...AND YET...

UH...
?
BKEEE

OH, P-CHAN!
I'M SO GLAD TO SEE YOU!
GYUU

NOW THIS IS RIDICULOUS...

IT'S ONE THING TO HAVE GREAT REFLEXES...
...BUT IF YOU CAN'T EVEN LET A HIGH SCHOOL GIRL...

--WAIT A SEC.
THAT ONE KICK...

...DID GET THROUGH HIS GUARD...
...BUT HOW...?!

gasp
CAN IT BE... ?!

I STILL DON'T UNDERSTAND, THOUGH.
STOP SQUIRMING, P-CHAN!
I HAVE TO WASH THAT DOODLE OFF YOU.
SHKK SHKK

GOSH, COULD IT BE...
SKHKK
SHKK
SHKK
SHKK
Peneton

I WISH YOU COULD TELL ME.
WHY WOULD YOU HAVE THE SAME DOODLE AS RYOGA?
B-BMP B-BMP

...THAT YOU'RE SECRETLY *RYOGA?*
KWEEE!
ISN'T THAT A SILLY IDEA?
RYOGA'S OFF ON A QUEST AND YOU'RE HERE.
NOD NOD
TIME TO WASH THE SOAP OFF...
...WITH SOME NICE *HOT WATER!*
DOOOOOM
BWEEEEK!

IF I'M RIGHT ABOUT THIS...

JUST HANG ON, RYOGA !
...WE CAN GET RID OF THAT FACE!

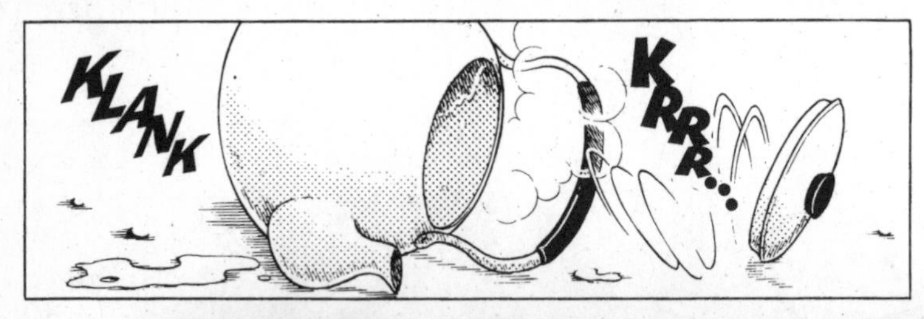
KRRR...
KLANK

NO...
STAGGER...
P-CHAN... ?!
Peng

PART 4
AKANE GUESSES THE SECRET!

I FIGURED OUT A WAY TO GET RID OF THAT MARK!
RYOGA! WHERE ARE YOU?!
SHTNG SHTNG

ERG.
HYUUUUUUUUUU...
WHA-- ?!
SHTNG
RYOGA'S BANDANNA...
AND A KETTLE ?!
SHTNG
Peneton

AKANE
!
Y-Y-YOU DIDN'T POUR WATER ON... ON...ON...

SHE *DID* IT!
SHE KNOWS...

I WAS... I WAS...
...J-JUST TRYING TO WASH THAT DOODLE OFF P-CHAN'S ST-STOMACH AND...

MIIIINNN MIINN
CHRP CHRP CHRP CHRP
AH, RYOGA...
I'M SORRY, MAN...

LISTEN...
IT MUST'VE BEEN A SHOCK TO YOU, BUT...

DON'T BLAME RYOGA.
HE NEVER MEANT TO HURT YOU...

BUT... WHAT'S RYOGA...
...HAVE TO DO WITH IT?
NEEP?
TIME TO WASH THE SOAP OFF WITH SOME NICE HOT WATER!
BWEEEK!

P-P-CHAN... NO!!
GLNK GLNK GLNK
GLNK GLNK
WHAT DOES RYOGA...

...HAVE TO DO WITH THAT?
gwi
.....

hsSh...

ZHEEE...
ZHEEE...
SLOSH
SLOSH

RANMA...
Y'KNOW...
YOU ARE ONE LUCKY MORON.
glg glg glg glg
BWEEEEK

YEAH.
IF MY THEORY IS CORRECT.
ARE YOU SERIOUS?! YOU CAN GET RID OF IT?!
MIIIINN
CHRP CHRP CHRP CHRP CHRP

OH, THERE YOU ARE, AKANE.
WHAT IS IT, KASUMI?

I WAS WONDERING IF YOU COULD HELP ME.
TODAY WE'RE...

ARE YOU SURE THIS IS GOING TO WORK?
tap tap

HEH. TALK ABOUT LUCKY!
WE CAN DO IT BEHIND THAT CURTAIN...

IT FINALLY HIT ME, AFTER FIGHTING YOU A COUPLE TIMES...
SHA

...THAT WHILE YOU WERE STANDING...
...YOU NEVER HAD ONE TINY OPENING IN YOUR DEFENSE.

BUT ONCE...
...WHEN THAT INCREDIBLY GRACEFUL, BEAUTIFUL GIRL HIT A VOLLEYBALL TO YOU...
...AND YOU CROUCHED TO HIT IT BACK...

YOU WERE OPEN !

WHICH MEANS...

OF COURSE !

THAT GIRL WAS *YOU!*
MNKH

DOES THAT MATTER *NOW?!*
THEN WHAT ARE YOU *SAYING ?!*

THIS, IDIOT...
THAT WHEN YOU CROUCHED, YOU CHANGED THE SHAPE OF THE MARKING...
...AND THAT MEANS...

...IF I CAN
CHANGE THIS
THING'S
EXPRESSION...

AND
THAT
MEANS...
IT WON'T
MAKE YOU
INVULNER-
ABLE.

THEN THE
MAGIC
SHOULD FADE
AWAY!
...I'LL BE ABLE
TO BEAT YOU
AS *USUAL!*
I
SEE...

DKONG

.....
HSSH

KWEE

KWEE

I THINK... YOU NEED... TO CHANGE IT...MORE...
I'M *TRYING*, BLAST YOU!
HOW ABOUT THIS ONE ?!
NOT GOOD ENOUGH !

KASUMI, ARE YOU READY YET?
ALMOST FINISHED, FATHER.

IT'S WEIRD...
WHAT WAS RANMA SO FREAKED ABOUT?

IT MUST'VE BEEN A SHOCK TO YOU, BUT...
...DON'T BLAME RYOGA.

WHAT IS IT... ?
WHAT'S GOING ON WITH RYOGA...?

ARRRGH! CAN'T YOU DO ANY-THING RIGHT?!
C'MON, STRETCH THAT THING!
MAKE LIKE AN OLD DRUNK WITH A BEER BELLY!

TWIST THAT STOMACH! TWIST! TWIST!
KREE KREE
NNNNRGH!

MORE! MORE!
NNGH!

WAHA-HAHAHA-HAHA!
WHAT'S SO FUNNY?!

THAT'S IT, FOOL!
YOU CAN DO IT!

DON'T LET ME DOWN, RANMA! NOW...
THIS TIME I'M *CLOBBERING* YOU!
STRIKE THE POSE!
NNNNNAAAGH!
GNNYUUUU
B-BUMP B-BUMP

SHAAAAAA

GASP
ULP.
KKK

HYUUUUUU
......

R... RYOGA...?

THE LADIES HAD TO RENT THE DOJO FOR THEIR MEETING...
UM...
WHO ARE THESE DAMES...?

LADIES' CLUB
tee hee hee
YADA YAMA YADA

WHICH ONE ?!
WEE-HA!
HOT STUFF THERE, SONNY!
WHAT A MAROON!
LOOK AT THAT STUPID FACE!
HA HA HA HA HA HA HA HA

TMP TMP
GO! GO! GO!
COME ON, BABY! SHAKE THAT THING!

HOO HOO HOO
I AM ONE...
BWA HA HA HA HA HA HA HA HA
FWEET FWEET FWEET
...UN-LUCKY MORON...

D-KONG

I WIN.
tweet tweet
FSSSSS...

LOOK! THE FACE IS VANISHING!
OOO!
A MAGIC SHOW!

THANK YOU VERY MUCH.
CLAP CLAP CLAP CLAP
FWEET FWEET
CLAP CLAP
CLAP CLAP
SO THAT'S THE SECRET!
tweet tweet

RYOGA WAS SECRETLY TRAINING TO ENTERTAIN THE LADIES' CLUB!

BUT WAIT A MINUTE...
chirrup
chirrup
chirrup

WHY DID P-CHAN HAVE THE SAME DOODLE AS RYOGA?

MAYBE RYOGA USED P-CHAN'S STOMACH FOR PRACTICE.

OH, THAT MAKES SENSE!
.....

AFTER ALL THE HELL RYOGA WENT THROUGH THIS TIME...
...HE'LL PROBABLY DISAPPEAR FOR A LONG WHILE...

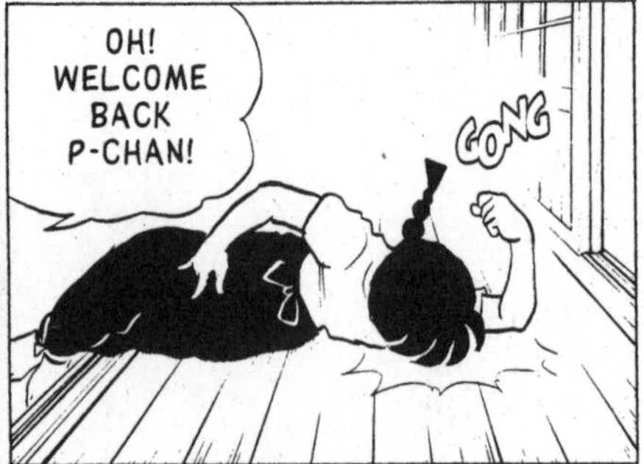
OH! WELCOME BACK P-CHAN!
GONG

AND THE DOODLE IS GONE.
I'M SO GLAD.
BWII
SOMETIMES I THINK BEING STUPID CAN BE A MAJOR ADVANTAGE...

PART 5
SANTA'S LITTLE DESCIPLES

BYE AKANE!
SEE YOU TOMORROW!
BYE-BYE!
HM?
COME ON, HANAKO, WE'RE ALMOST THERE.
BUT I'M TOO TIRED.
WHAT'S WRONG?
OH... WE'RE... UM...
CARROT
...LOOKING FOR THIS OLD MAN.

......
KILL KILL KILL KILL KILL KILL KILL
PANTY THIEF !
SHING SHING SHING
CARROT

YOO HOO, AKANE !
BYOING

WILL YOU QUIT *BUGGIN'* PEOPLE?!
BONK

EEEEE
YEEEEE-E
DOMP BOMP

MUTTER MUTTER
HYUUUU
HMMM...

WHAT DO YOU WANT WITH THIS HORRIBLE OLD MAN?
DID HE STEAL SOME-THING FROM YOU?
HUH?
CARROT

STEAL?!
SANTA DOESN'T STEAL!
WE FOUND HIM! WE FOUND SANTA!

Y...
YOU MEAN YOU'RE...
WE CAME TO SEE YOU! JUST LIKE WE PROMISED!
OKAY, HAPPOSAI...
...WHAT THE HECK IS THIS?!
AHEM

WELL ... THIS PAST CHRISTMAS EVE...
POING
POING
DECK THE HALLS WITH BRAS AND PANTIES...
...ON MY WAY HOME FROM MY NIGHTLY ROUNDS...

DO YOU WANT TO HAVE CHRISTMAS WITH ME?
AH, POOR DARLINGS...
POING
gwii

...I SAW A LONELY PAIR OF STOCKINGS, HUNG BY A WINDOW WITH CARE...

SHOOP
FWAP

TWONG
DONK

AN' HE BROUGHT ME SOME UNDIES!
WE CAUGHT SANTA CLAUS!
WE DID IT, HANAKO!

HOW COULD I DISILLUSION TWO INNOCENT TYKES?
PSS PSS
...YOU WENT ALONG WITH IT?!

YOU MEAN...

AND WHEN THEY TOLD ME THEIR FATHER WAS OUT OF TOWN...
...AND THEIR MOTHER WOULDN'T BE HOME UNTIL LATE...
...I JUST FELT SO SORRY FOR THEM!
WOO HOO HOO HOO! MORE CHICKEN!
MORE CAKE! MORE SAKE!!
ALL I WANTED WAS TO BRING THEM CHRISTMAS CHEER.
UH HUH. TELL ME ANOTHER ONE.

MURRAY KISHMASH...
...'N T'WALL A G'NIGH.
pik pik
SANTA, WAIT!
I WANT TO BE YOUR HELPER WHEN I GROW UP.
CAN'T YOU TEACH ME HOW?

BWAHAHAHAHA! COME SEE ME ANYTIME AN' I'LL MAKE YOU MY DISCIPLE!
I WILL, I WILL !
BWUH

O-KAY... AND NOW...?
I DIDN'T THINK THEY'D ACTUALLY FIND ME!
BUT SANTA, ON THE PRESENT YOU GAVE US...
......
YOU WRITE YOUR ADDRESS...ON YOUR STOLEN UNDERWEAR?!
NERIMA'S TENDO DOJO
bonk

YOU PROMISED, SANTA! MAKE ME YOUR DISCIPLE!
I'LL DO ANYTHING! I DON'T CARE HOW HARD IT IS!

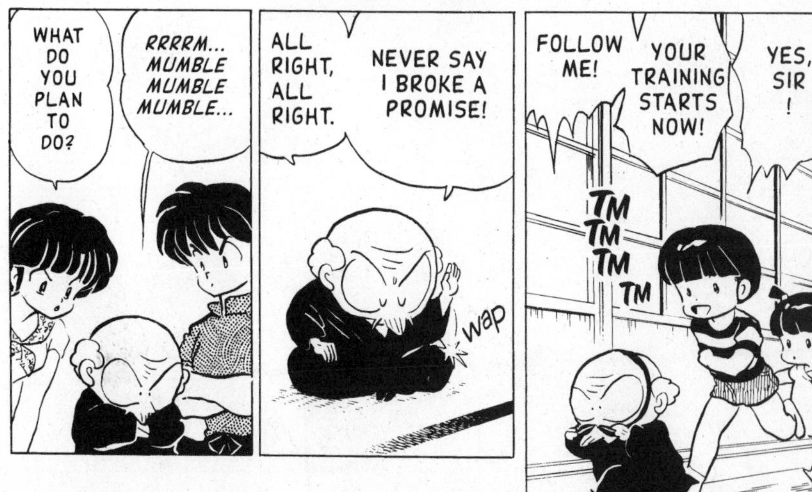
WHAT DO YOU PLAN TO DO?
RRRRM... MUMBLE MUMBLE MUMBLE...
ALL RIGHT, ALL RIGHT.
NEVER SAY I BROKE A PROMISE!
wap
FOLLOW ME!
YOUR TRAINING STARTS NOW!
YES, SIR!
TM TM TM TM

THE FIRST RULE OF SANTAHOOD!
NEVER LET YOURSELF BE SEEN!
YES SIR!

SNEAK

HYOI

FWIP
FWIP FWIP

HEY.
MOOF!!

WHAT'RE YOU PULLING?
WE'RE GATHERING PRESENTS, OF COURSE!

MERRY CHRISTMAS!
STF STF STF
HOLD IT, YOU--

SHOOP
urk
D-KONG
SECOND RULE!
KNOW YOUR WAY AROUND CHIMNEYS!
BATH HOUSE

BLOOSH
HSSSSH

SPLASH

BGGYNNG
STOP *RIGHT* THERE.

YOU AGAIN!
NO PRESENTS FOR *YOU* THIS YEAR, YOUNG MAN!
JUST *WHAT* DO YOU THINK YOU'RE TEACHING THESE KIDS?!

NOW LISTEN, KIDS...
IF YOU THINK THIS IS REALLY *SANTA*, YOU NEED TO LEARN A FEW--

HAVE YOU NO RESPECT FOR *INNOCENCE* ?!
WAK !
TONG

IT'S NOT WHAT IT *LOOKS* LIKE!
EEEEEEEEEEEEEEEEEE...

FEH.
AMATEURS...
DONK
BONNK
eeek
eeek
THE THIRD LAW!
BE QUICK ON YOUR FEET!
RAMEN
GLMP GLMP GLMP GLMP GLMP GLMP GLMP

THERE'S NO BETTER WAY TO BUILD STRONG LEGS AND LOSE...

STOP! THE CHECK !
...AFTER EATING !!
VSSH

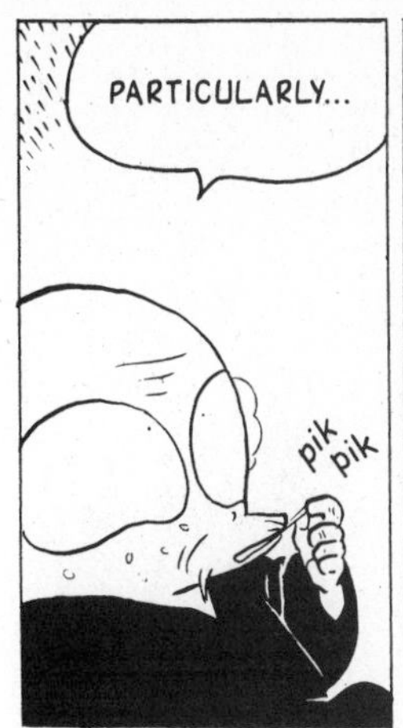
PARTICULARLY...
pik pik

EH ?
HYUUUUUU
RAMEN
STATIONERY
Cafe
PAWN SHOP
Ramen

.....
ONE TWO THREE
IS IT ENOUGH ?
CHIK CHIK

G'CHAKK
KSSHH

YEAH...
DO YOU THINK...
MAYBE SANTA'S POOR ?

...TO BUY PRESENTS FOR OTHERS.
HE MUST BE USING ALL HIS MONEY...
RATTLE

RRRRRGH!!
THAT... SICK... OLD... FREAK...
SHF-KLMP SHF-KLMP

WHAT'S THE FOURTH RULE, SANTA?
HUH?

SUCH... INNOCENCE...
NGH!
TWINKLE TWINKLE

EVERY DISCIPLE I'VE EVER HAD...
...HAS TREATED ME WITH SUCH DIS-RESPECT...
...UNTIL NOW...

THIS IS THE FIRST TIME...
...I'VE EVER BEEN TRULY UNDERSTOOD... AND TREATED WITH THE KINDNESS I DESERVE!

GYURRRNG
TRUST ME. YOU NEVER GOT *HALF* WHAT YOU DESERVE!

OH, PLEASE, SIR! STOP HURTING SANTA CLAUS!
.....

IS THERE ANY CONSCIENCE IN THERE AT ALL?
PAP PAP
FEH...

I'LL SHOW YOU CONSCIENCE!
GRRRRRR
THE FOURTH LAW!
DO GOOD *DEEDS*!!

WHAT KINDA GOOD DEEDS, SANTA?!
TWINKLE TWINKLE

UM... YES...
GOOD DEEDS...
GOOD DEEDS...

GOO... GOO... GOO-WOOO...
GNYEE

BOOM
SHORTED HIMSELF OUT, EH?

YOU NEVER HAD ALL THIS TROUBLE...
...'TIL YOU TRIED TEACHING US...
HE FINALLY WENT TOO FAR...
WE'RE LUCKY HE DIDN'T TRY TO DO A GOOD DEED...
HE MIGHT HAVE BLOWN US ALL UP.
POOR SANTA...
OOOG
NNNNGH
URRRGLE

IT'S IN HERE...
OH, BUT...
WE BROUGHT YOU A PRESENT...
WE GIVE UP BEING YOUR DISCIPLES.
WE'VE LEARNED OUR LESSON.
UH...?

WE KNOW YOU LOVE UNDER-WEAR, SO...

P-P-PANTIES!
PING
IT'S A MIRACLE!
POING

THEY'RE MY DAD'S...
I HOPE THEY'RE NOT TOO BIG.
BOOM

WE HOPE YOU GET BETTER SOON!
EVEN HE HAS HIS LIMITS...
THE FINAL BLOW...
SSS...

I GUESS I'LL NEVER GET TO BE SANTA'S HELPER.
I DIDN'T KNOW IT WOULD BE SO HARD.

EVEN BETTER THAN SANTA WAS DOING!
YOU SURE CAN.
BUT YOU CAN STILL DO GOOD DEEDS.

I WOULDN'T COUNT ON IT.
DON'T YOU THINK EVEN HAPPOSAI HAS TO FEEL JUST A LITTLE BAD ABOUT THIS?

HUH ?
HYURURURU
LOOKA ME!

PAP
IT'S A SANTA FIRE-BURST !

BE GOOD, CHILDREN !
POOOOOOM
AND YOUR STOCKINGS WILL BE FULL THIS YEAR!
OH SANTA... !

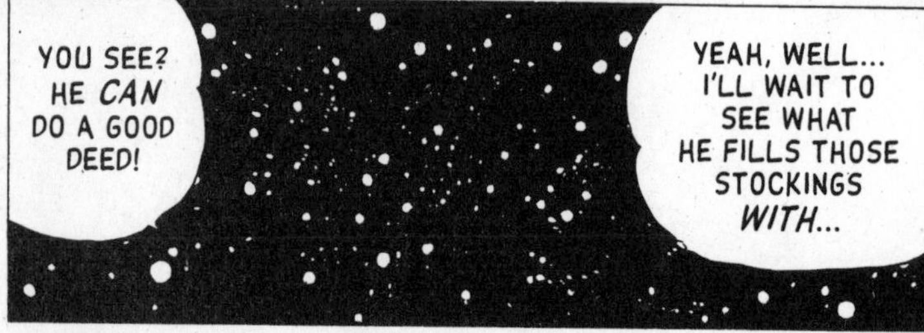
YOU SEE? HE CAN DO A GOOD DEED!
YEAH, WELL... I'LL WAIT TO SEE WHAT HE FILLS THOSE STOCKINGS WITH...

PART 6
WHEN YOU WISH UPON A SWORD

SPECIAL DELIVERY !
FOR AKANE TENDO AND... "THE PIGTAILED GIRL"?!
FOR ME AND RANMA... ?
WHO'S IT FROM ?
RRIP RRIP
WHO ELSE WOULD ADDRESS IT TO "THE PIG-TAILED GIRL"?! KUNO!

IT'S HEAVY...
fmp
RIP RIP
HUH ?

HHHHHH...

AKANE TENDO...
PIGTAILED GIRL...
I WILL BE UNABLE TO ATTEND SCHOOL FOR THE NEXT THREE DAYS, DUE TO... PERSONAL REASONS. HEH HEH.
VNNNNNNN...
SOMETIMES I WISH BAD TASTE WAS A *CRIME*.
ZH ZH

YOU WILL BE LONELY, I KNOW.
THAT IS WHY I SEND YOU THIS STATUE...
...THAT YOU MAY GAZE LOVINGLY UPON IT UNTIL I RETURN TO Y-
FZZT
GOMP

GONNNNG
WAIT IN LINE, GENTLEMEN!
I'M SURE YOU'LL ALL HAVE A CHANCE TO TRY DRAWING OUT THE *WISH-BRINGER*.
MRMR MRMR
GRMBL GRMBL
BAH. WHAT FOOLS THEY ARE...
...GATHERING HERE ON THIS DAY EVERY YEAR, HOPING TO MAKE THE SACRED BLADE THEIR OWN.

AND YET, SINCE FEUDAL DAYS IT HAS SAT...
...TRAPPED WITHIN ITS STONE, TANTALIZING WITH ITS SHINING PROMISE...

...THAT WHEN FINALLY DRAWN...
...IT WILL GRANT ITS LIBERATOR THREE WISHES!

THE GREATEST WARRIORS OF HISTORY HAVE TRIED...
...ONLY TO FIND THEMSELVES UNEQUAL TO THE TASK.

AND NOW, THESE MODERN WEAKLINGS...
MRMR
MRMR
NKH NKH NKH NKH NKH NKH.
NOT TODAY, YOUNG MAN! HO HO HO.

NO STRENGTH OR SKILL CAN FREE THE WISHBRINGER.

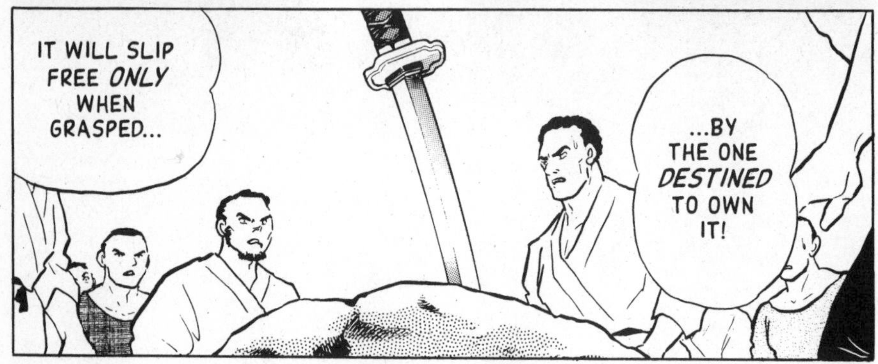
IT WILL SLIP FREE *ONLY* WHEN GRASPED...
...BY THE ONE *DESTINED* TO OWN IT!

NNNN-NNNG-YARH!!
THANK YOU. NEXT!
HNNN-GWU-HH!!
CAW CAW
LOVELY. NEXT!
NEX...
TMP
OH!
M-M-MASTER... IF THE PR-PROPHECIES ARE *TRUE*, TH-THEN...
IS IT POSSIBLE...?

ACCORDING TO THIS SCROLL PASSED DOWN THROUGH THE AGES...
YES! THERE IS NO DOUBT!

HE IS THE WISHBRINGER'S CHOSEN!
THIS MAN IS HE!

SHHHHH...
OOOH!

...MY DESTINY ?!
GNG

C-CAN THIS TRULY BE...
YADA YADA

IT IS DONE!
THE WISH-BRINGER HAS BEEN CLAIMED AT LAST!
CAW CAW
ARK ARK
CAW CAW

A SACRED BLADE THAT GRANTS THREE WISHES...
THREE... WISHES...
HMMM...
THIS IS A PROBLEM.
AFTER ALL...
I'M GORGEOUS! I'M BRILLIANT! I'M RICH!
I EVEN HAVE A GREAT PERSONALITY!
WHAT AM I GOING TO DO WITH THREE WISHES?!
PSS PSS
Let's go around...

HEY KUNO, WELCOME BACK!
SO WHERE WERE YA?
MNSH
HEH...
WISH-BRINGER!
NUMBER ONE!
SHK
EEK!
A REAL SWORD!
HUMBLE THIS FOOL!
YOUR WISH IS MY COMMAND.
gasp

AND RANMA...
HUH? IZZAT KUNO?
THE SWORD... IT TALKED!
FOR RENT
HEH.
HYAAAAA
PREPARE YOURSELF!
EEEEEE!
YOU THINK I'M AFRAID OF SOME CHEAP SWORD?!
SHA
AN OPENING!
DOMM!
BWONG
WHA?!

IT IS DONE...
TA-DAAA
ARE YOU OKAY, RANMA?
BWOOP
NNNNGH...
NOW YOU KNOW...
...NEVER TO CHALLENGE MY PROWESS AGAIN.
ching
THAT SWORD...
...WHAT WAS IT?

MRMR MRMR
HMM...
POST NO BEARS

Correct me if I'm wrong...
...but that looks like the Wishbringer!

THE ONE MAN DESTINED TO DRAW IT?
YOU ?
THERE MUST BE SOME MISTAKE.
FEH.
IF YOU DON'T BELIEVE ME...

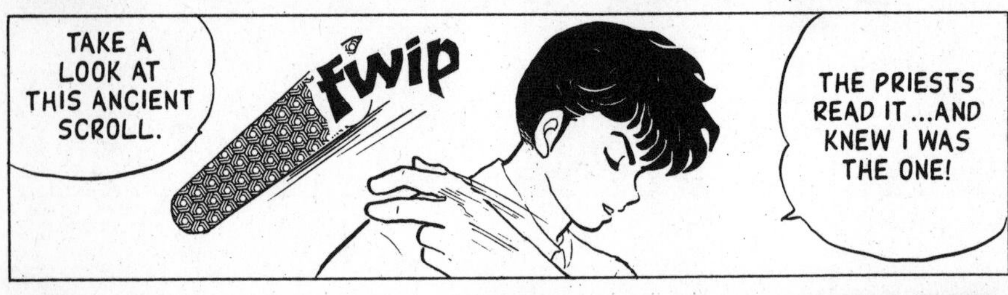
TAKE A LOOK AT THIS ANCIENT SCROLL.
fwip
THE PRIESTS READ IT ...AND KNEW I WAS THE ONE!

FWA
WH-WHAT THE... ?
.....
WHAT IS THIS ?
WELL...

SPANG
CONGRATULATIONS! YOU'RE OUR ONE MILLIONTH SWORD-PULLER!
CLAP CLAP CLAP CLAP
CLAP CLAP CLAP
AARGH! OF ALL THE LUCK!
BAH!
I SHALL NEVER FORGET THAT FEELING OF... PRIDE!
SOBB
WELL...
I GUESS IT'S LIKE WINNING THE LOTTERY.
OKAY, SO HOWEVER HE GOT IT...
...HE'S STILL GOT TWO WISHES LEFT, RIGHT?
HEH...

MY SECOND WISH IS CLEAR...
SHK
WITH THE POWER OF THE WISH-BRINGER...
NYAH HAH—HAH HAH HAH HAH HAH
...I CAN TAKE OVER THE WORLD!
WE GOTTA GET THAT SWORD AWAY FROM HIM!
AAAAAA!

YOUR WISH IS MY COMMAND.
I WISH TO DATE THE PIGTAILED GIRL!
BOOOOM
THANK GOD...
YEAH... THANK GOD HE'S AN IDIOT...
WHEW...

NO KIDDING.
NO KIDDING, POPS?
A SWORD THAT GRANTS WISHES?!

IF WE GET THAT SWORD... WE GET THOSE WISHES!
NOW LISTEN...

TH-THEN... THAT WOULD MEAN...

I'D NEVER HAVE TO BE A PANDA AGAIN!
I'D NEVER HAVE TO BE A GIRL AGAIN!
SHOOOOOM

sponk
HUH?
A MESSAGE?

My beloved Kuno,
Please, please won't you ask me out again?
Forever yours,
The Pigtailed Girl.
BLAM
WAAAH!! ALREADY?!

HEH HEH HEH...ENJOY IT WHILE YOU CAN, FOOL!
POP
WISH-BRINGER, I LOVE YOU!

PART 7
MAY I CUT IN?

YOU CAN'T BE SERIOUS!
GOING OUT... WITH KUNO?!

THAT MAGIC SWORD HE'S GOT...
...CAME OUT OF THE ROCK WITH THREE WISHES IN IT!

FROM WHAT I HEAR...
KUNO'S ALREADY USED TWO OF THOSE...
WHICH MEANS YOU'VE GOT TO GET IT QUICKLY...BEFORE HE USES THE LAST WISH!
RELAX, POPS. IT'S A DONE DEAL.
HECK, I'LL EVEN...
FOR THE CHANCE TO BE ALL-MALE, ALL THE TIME...
GRNCH

Teeheeheeheehee
...BE THE PRETTIEST LI'L THING YOU EVER SAW!
THAT'S MY BOY!
.....
THE FAIR!
THE MOVIES!
THE CAFE!
I'LL HAVE ALL THE CHANCES I NEED!

PFF.
RANMA, YOU ARE SO NAIVE.
NABIKI... ?
YOU THINK A DATE WITH KUNO...
...IS GONNA GO THAT SMOOTHLY?
TRUE...
IT IS KUNO...
BWOOOO
OH, SHOOT! WE MISSED THE LAST TRAIN.
GEE, I'M A LITTLE TIPSY!
HERE.
THIS WILL TAKE CARE OF YOU!
SHA
KNOCK-OUT DROPS
SHF SHF

fmp
NYAHAHAHAHA! SO, YOU WANT THE WISHBRINGER, DO YOU?!
EEEEK!
RRRRRIP
BRRRRRR! THE HORROR!
HEY.
LEAVE ME OUTTA YOUR SICK FANTASIES, OKAY?
OH, RANMA... POOR RANMA...
YOU NEED LIPSTICK.
SO, YOU THINK A MINI-SKIRT IS BETTER?

twee twee
tk tk tk
SHNAWW
GRSNX
TM TM TM TM TM TM TM
GOOD MORNING, PIGTAILED GIRL!
TOOM
ZHOOP
LET US BE OFF!
GNAH ?

DN DN DN DN DN DN DN
WHAT IS IT ?!
IT MUST BE A THIEF!

WHA
WHA
WHA...

HA HA HA! WHO'S A LITTLE SLEEPY-HEAD, HM?
TUNK

DO YOU HAVE *ANY* IDEA... WHAT *TIME* IT IS?
MNSH

KUNO ?! WH... WHAT... ?

AH! DEAREST AKANE!

FORGIVE ME.
FOR TODAY... I BELONG TO THE PIG-TAILED GIRL.

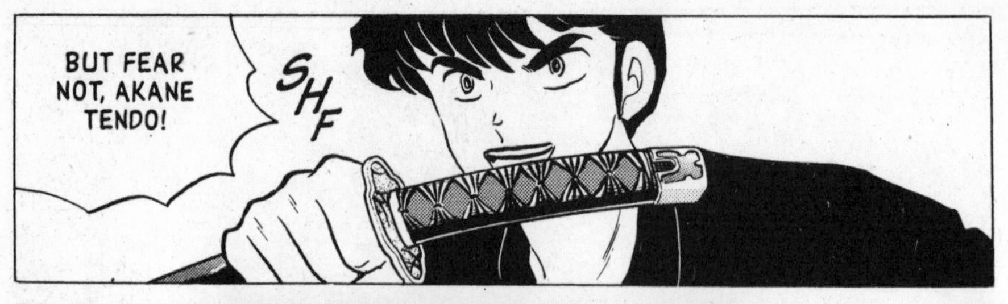
BUT FEAR NOT, AKANE TENDO!
SHF

FOR MY FINAL WISH...
ping
NO NO NO NO NO NO!!

...I'LL WISH FOR A DATE WITH Y--
I'M READY! WHATCHA WAITIN' FOR?
MONK

SHHHH...

HOW GRAND TO WITNESS THE BIRTH OF A NEW DAY!
AH!
NAMAN DAMA NAMAN DAMA
OOOO, SO PRETTY!

WAIT A MINUTE.
IF THERE'S ONLY ONE WISH LEFT...

THEN MY ONLY CHOICE...
I'LL RACE YOU TO THE LIGHTHOUSE! *HO HO HO!*
COME, PIGTAILED GIRL!
SHF
SHF

POP... OR ME...
ONLY ONE OF US...
...CAN BECOME NORMAL AGAIN!

THIS IS FIRST COME, FIRST SERVED!
SHA
...IS TO SAY, "SORRY, POP!"

VVSSSHHHH...

WHAT'S THE *IDEA*, FATHER DEAR?
TO GET THAT LAST WISH... *DAUGHTER* DEAR!
WELL, THAT MAKES IT EASY!
BONK

SPLASSSSSH
YOO-HOO, KUNO! WAIT FOR LI'L *ME-EEE!*

.....
YOU THINK A DATE WITH KUNO...
...IS GONNA GO THAT SMOOTHLY?
hssh!
I'M STILL PLANNING TO KEEP AN EYE ON THEM...
BUT SOMEHOW I DON'T THINK I HAVE MUCH TO WORRY ABOUT...

HO HOHO HOHO !
YOU'RE FALLING BEHIND, PIGTAILED GIRL!
BUT KUNO, YOU RUN SO FAST! *TEE HEE!*
ZHAA
ZHAA
ZHAA
ZHAA

EEK !
SHWUMP

PIG-TAILED GIRL...

ARE YOU ALL RIGHT!?
SHMP

GOTCHA GOTCHA GOTCHA!
TEE HEE HEE!
SKWEEZ
OH...P-PIGTAILED GIRL...

HSS
THAT SWORD...IS *MINE!!*

fmp...
NOW, NOW, NOW, MY LITTLE PIG-TAILED PRETTY!
GWOM
A LADY SHOULDN'T BE SO FORWARD!
AAA!
AAA!
MY DIARY

OH, KUNO... YOU'RE S-S-SUCH A G-GENTLE-MAN...
A TRUE RELATIONSHIP IS BASED ON SHARED INTIMACIES! PLEASE... READ MY DIARY!
HOO HOO HOO

THANKS FOR THE TIP, AKANE!
SHA
KNOCKOUT DROPS
I MADE IT ALL MYSELF!
ISN'T IT DELICIOUS?
OH, KUNO, YOU'RE WONDERFUL!
HO HO HO
NOW WE WILL HAVE LUNCH!

SHF
SHF

SAY "AHHH."
GLOP

I...I HOPE...
...THAT WASN'T TOO FORWARD OF ME...
BLUSH

EH ?
SHNAWW

TAKING A NAP !
HOW SWEET !

YES.
AND SO HEALTHY, TOO.
HHSSHHHHHHHHHHHH

OF COURSE...
ONE L-L-L-LITTLE K-K-K-KISS W-WON'T HURT ANY...

AND *THIS* ISN'T *"FORWARD"* ?!
GONG

RANMA !
WHAT DO YOU THINK YOU'RE DOING!?
SPLASH
HWAH ?

IT'S *MINE! MINE!*
GWAAAAAAH!!
VROOM

COME BACK HERE, YOU CROOK!

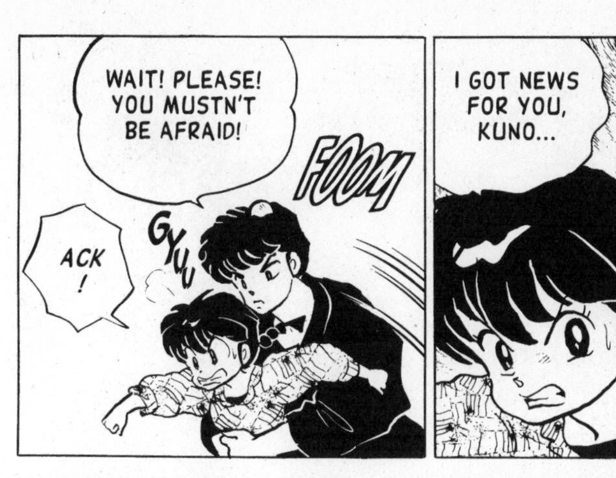
WAIT! PLEASE! YOU MUSTN'T BE AFRAID!
FOOM
GYUU
ACK!
I GOT NEWS FOR YOU, KUNO...

I'M NOT!!
BOOT

WISH-BRINGER... I COMMAND YOU...
SHHA
NO.

...FREE ME OF THE PANDA!
KRAK

BZZT.
VOICE CHECK NOT VERIFIED.
YOUR WISH IS INVALID.

AH-HAH!
SO THE ONLY ONE IT GRANTS WISHES TO IS ITS *OWNER*!
WHAT?!

TH-THEN THAT MEANS...
DNK

ALL I HAVE TO DO IS ASK MY DARLING KUNO TO MAKE THE WISH *FOR* ME!
tee hee
......

HERE, KUNO! I BROUGHT BACK YOUR LI'L SWORDIE-SWORD!
AH, THANK YOU!
BOO HOO HOO
MAYBE I *DO* HAVE SOMETHING TO WORRY ABOUT AFTER ALL...

PART 8
THE FINAL WISH

TEE-HEE HEE! CATCH ME IF YOU CA-A-A-AN!
HAHA-HAHA-HA!
COME BACK HERE, YOU!

I SHALL HAVE THE *WISHBRINGER* MAKE IT SO!
I WANT YOU TO WISH AWAY A FEMININE PROBLEM OF MINE!
I *DON'T* THINK IT'LL BE THAT EASY...

I GUESS KUNO'S THE OUTDOORSY TYPE.
FIRST THE BEACH... NOW THE MOUNTAINS...
VIP

...I CAN'T BELIEVE EVEN *RANMA* COULD PULL THIS OFF!
BUT STILL...

YOU JUST WATCH! WITH MY FEMININE WILES...
...I'LL HAVE HIM BEGGIN' TO USE THAT WISH ON ME!

COME HERE, YOU!
HUHH HUHH
EEEEK!
Y-YOU'RE SO... FAST!
ZHEE ZHEE
EEEEK!

ALL RIGHT!
HSSH
I'LL WISH THAT I CAN CATCH YOU!
BWOK
DON'T BE WASTING THE WISH ON IDIOCY... IDIOT!

HAHAHA! I'M ONLY KIDDING.
OH, YOU SILLY!
tee hee

SAY, YOU ONLY HAVE ONE WISH LEFT, RIGHT?

YOU SHOULD SAVE IT FOR SOMETHING IMPORTANT.
BUT OF COURSE!

YOU MUST BE TIRED FROM ALL THAT RUNNING!

I'LL HAVE THE MAGIC SWORD BRING US A CAFE!
HSS
H
DON'T YOU *DARE*!!

Tweet
SSHH

WHAT?! A PROBLEM, YOU SAY?!
CHR CHR
VISTA POINT

REALLY ?
I'M SURE I CAN HELP!

IT'S ABOUT MY BODY...
W- WELL...
sigh

IT'S A PROMISE, THEN !
I AM A MAN OF MY WORD!

I DO !
BUT IF YOU SAY SO...
HSS

I THINK YOU'RE FINE JUST AS YOU ARE.
REALLY ?
OGLE OGLE

THAT'S NOT *IT!!*
WISHBRINGER... BRING THE PIGTAILED GIRL BIGGER B--

NOW LET US GO AND FIND SOME LUNCH!
HAHAHA, ISN'T THIS FUN?
RANMA TALKED BIG...BUT IT'S KUNO WHO'S CALLING THE SHOTS!

AHHH...
SAY "AHH..."
HERE YOU ARE!
.....

SSSH
Bed & Breakfast

I DON'T KNOW HOW MUCH LONGER I CAN HOLD OUT, IF I DON'T GET SOME RESULTS...
THIS IS SO LAME...

I DIDN'T WANNA HAVE TO RESORT TO THIS...BUT I GOTTA START LAYING ON THE CHARM!

OH, KU-U-UNO...
PRRR PRRR
P-PIGTAILED GIRL...!

WHAT--?
WHAT'S HE DOING...?

IF YOU USE THAT LI'L OL' SWORD ON MY WISH...

I'LL DO ANNNY-THING YOU WANT ME TO!
B-BOOOM

"A-A-A-A-N-N-NY-TH-THING"?!
B-BMP B-BMP
B-BMP

GWAAAP
RANMA!
HAVE YOU NO *SHAME*?!
boo hoo
YOU SADDEN YOUR FATHER, BOY...

AKA-KA-KANE... TEN-ENDO...
WHAT'S *SHE* GOT TO DO WITH IT?!

SHE CAME ALL THIS WAY AFTER ME...
SIGH
SHE IS SO JEALOUS OF THE PIG-TAILED GIRL...

SO IN *LOVE* WITH ME!
MNSH
YOU *WISH*!

STAY *OUTTA* THIS, AKANE!
ARE YOU *THAT* DESPERATE TO STOP BEING A GIRL?!

YOU DON'T KNOW THE HALF OF IT!
COME *ON*, KUNO!
TMP TMP TMP TMP
FORGIVE ME, AKANE TENDO!
GET *BACK* HERE!

RAN-
MAA
!!
TM
TM
TM
TM

I CAN HIDE IN THAT WATERFALL...
PSH
PSH
PSH
PSH

.....
WE'RE SAFE IN HERE, KUNO.
HEH HEH
I LOST THEM...
ERG...
PSH
PSH
PSH
PSH
WORLD-FAMOUS
HOT-WATER FALLS

HRRRRRRR
R-R-
RANMA...
SAO...TO...
ME...!
HUH
?

*OH...
BOY
OH
BOY...*

WHERE...
DID YOU
HIDE...

...THE
PIGTAILED
GIRL!!
VWOOP
VWOOP

WAIT...
OF
COURSE
!
WHAT
COULD
MATTER
MORE...

WISHBRINGER!
FIND ME THE
PIGTAILED--
BONK
FIRE
BCOSH
SILLY! YOU
DON'T NEED
A WISH FOR
THAT!
CANDIES
SOUVENIRS

HNSH
OH... KUNO!
OH, PIGTAILED GIRL, HOW I'VE MISSED YOU!

I'VE ALMOST GOT HIM...

TH-TH-THEN...
CL-CLOSE YOUR EYES...

ANYTHING, KUNO!
I'LL DO IT!
AB-B-BOUT WHAT YOU SAID...

OUR FIRST DATE... OUR FIRST KISS...
SIGH
OH, HOW LUCKY I AM!
HEH HEH HEH...
PAP PAP
IF YOU WANT IT THAT BADLY...
I WON'T STOP YOU.

GO AHEAD AND K-KISS HIM!
YOU HAVE YOUR F-FATHER'S BL-BL-BLESSING!
DID I ASK FOR IT ?!

YEAH. GO AHEAD.
I WON'T STOP YOU EITHER.
AKA-KANE TENDO !
DON'T WORRY !
I'LL BE HAPPY TO KISS YOU SOON AS I'M THROUGH KISSING--
DON'T BOTHER !

ZHA

...AND I'LL BE A MAN AGAIN!!
GWEE

THAT'S ALL...
ONE MOMENT OF HORROR...

OH, RANMA... YOU FOOL!

RANMA...
?

D'KLONNG
AAAUGH
!
I CAN'T
DO IT!

OWEE...
THIS
DATE...
I JUST...
PLAIN...
CAN'T!
ZZHH

HOLD,
PIG-
TAILED
GIRL!
BORP
BORP
HWIP
...IS
NOW
OVER
!!

HUH...
?
I TRULY...
TRULY...
...ENJOYED
OUR DATE
TODAY.

FROM THE BEGINNING, I HAD INTENDED TO GIVE YOU THE FINAL WISH AS A GIFT...
heh

VWI

NOW COMES THE FINAL WISH!
WISH-BRINGER !

YOU... YOU INTENDED...
YOU WHAT ?!

HOW COULD I MISJUDGE HIM?
OH, KUNO...

YOUR WISH IS MY COMMAND.
BLAAAAM!
IN MEMORY OF THE FIRST DATE OF TATEWAKI KUNO AND THE PIGTAILED GIRL

WELL, IT *IS* A LOVELY LITTLE STATUE...
KUNO SAID HE COULD TELL JUST WHAT THE PIGTAILED GIRL WANTED MOST...
THIS IS WHAT YOU WANTED, RANMA?
NOOOOO!!!
BETTER THAN I EVER GOT.

PART 9
THE KING IS WILD

OKONOMIYAKI
Ucchan's
FWSH
CLOSED
SH
SH
OKAY--
ANOTHER
DAY AT
THE SALT
MINES.
KWRR
OPEN
SHMM
DANGER
?!
EH
?

SHAA
WHO'S
THERE
!?

PSH
PSH
FSSSHH
PLAYING CARDS ?
EH ?

WHAT ARE YOU SAYING ?!
VOO
YOU LOSE, UKYO...
HEH HEH HEH...

A ROYAL FLUSH !!
VWA
THIS !

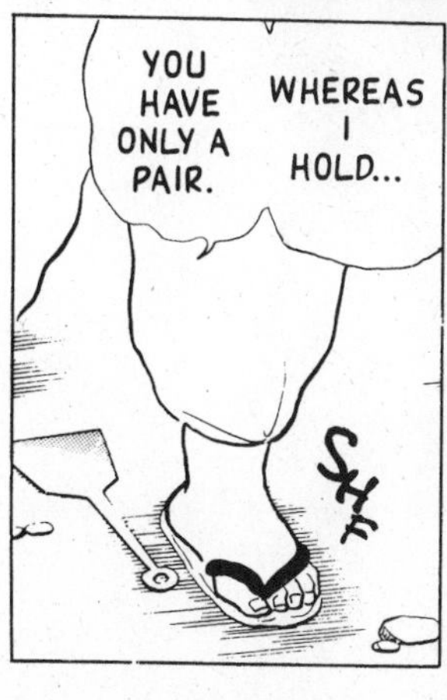

WHEREAS I HOLD...
YOU HAVE ONLY A PAIR.
SHF

RRRRRR...
MONG...
NOW WHO IN HECK *ARE* YOU?!
GOOD FOR YOU.

YOU'RE... YOU'RE...
YOU...

"GAMBLING KING"... ?
THE GAMBLING KING?! HE'S BACK?!

...FOR WHEN IT COMES TO GAMES OF CHANCE...
SO HE IS KNOWN...
Artist's Impression
南
北
東
一萬
...HE IS SAID TO BE UNBEATABLE !!

...TO PAY US BACK FOR WHAT WE DID!!
HE'S COME BACK...

IT'S ABOUT THAT DEBT FROM TEN YEARS AGO...
WHY WOULD RANMA KNOW A GAMBLER...?

SNAKE-EYE !
HWYU

ZONG

AND A *BOXCAR* FOR YOU, RANMA...
HEH HEH HEH!
FIP

YOU SHOULD HAVE KNOWN BETTER...
...THAN TO TRY YOUR LUCK AGAINST THE GAMBLING KING!
VWAA

FOR TEN YEARS...
520 WEEKS...
3,653 DAYS...
...I HAVE WAITED TO DEFEAT YOU.
YOU SHOULD FEEL HONORED!

I CAN'T BEGIN TO TELL YOU...
MNSH

WHAT COULD HAVE HAPPENED BETWEEN THEM...
...WHEN RANMA WAS SO YOUNG...?

いろは
TEN YEARS AGO...
WHEE WHEE
AUTUMN FESTIVAL
...I WAS RUNNING MY BUSINESS AS USUAL...
YOU LOSE !
RRG

...WHEN...
WAIT JUST A MINUTE !
FWEE
ARE YOU THE ONE WHO'S BEEN TAKING ALL THESE KIDS' MONEY?

THE GAME ?
I ACCEPT.

YOU AND ME...ONE-ON-ONE?
HOW 'BOUT IT?

I FELT NO FEAR. OLD MAID WAS THE FIRST GAME I'D MASTERED.
OLD MAID !!

ONE MORE !
YOU LOSE !

ONE MORE GAME!
YOU LOSE.

AAAK !!
YOU LOSE !
JOKER

IT WAS MY SWEETEST VICTORY!
HA HA HA HA...
AND THEN... ?

NO PROBLEM.
RAN-CHAN! GET HIM FOR ME!
I'D LOST MY DAD'S FAST-FOOD BUSINESS TO HIM...SO...
Entitles Bearer to ownership of My Okonomiyaki cart.
Signed, Ukyo Kuonji

GAMBLING KING! PREPARE TO MEET YOUR MATCH!
POPCORN

AAAK!!
YOU LOSE.

ONE MORE GAME!
YOU LOSE.
ONE MORE!
YOU LOSE.

EEE-YAARG!
BONNNG
FOOLISH CHILD.
YOU HAVE NOTHING LEFT TO WAGER.

YES I DO!
HERE'S THE DEED!
VWA
VERY GENEROUS OF YOU.

AT THAT POINT...
...FINDING MYSELF AT THE END OF MY ROPE...
WE WRAPPED HIM UP LIKE SUSHI AND DUMPED HIM IN THE RIVER.
YOU... WHAT ?!

NO *WONDER* HE HATES YOU SO MUCH!
YOU SEE?! I'M THE *VICTIM* HERE!

OH. THE "VICTIM," EH...?
LOOK! HE DROPPED HIS CARDS!
WAIT A SECOND...
THEY'RE ALL *JOKERS* !
JOKER
HE WAS *CHEATING* !

WHAT KINDA "VICTIM" CHEATS LITTLE KIDS OUT OF THEIR MONEY?!
FEH...
MNSH

HAVE YOU FORGOTTEN ?
I STILL HOLD THE PAPERS!
SMIRK

I HEARD THE WHOLE STORY.
DAD...?
VP

IF YOU MADE AN AGREEMENT, YOU MUST LIVE UP TO IT.
RANMA...
HAND OVER WHATEVER YOU PROMISED HIM
...AND HAVE HIM GO ON HIS WAY.

HEY, JUST BECAUSE IT'S NO SKIN OFF *YOUR* NOSE...

HUH ?
Entitles Bearer to ownership of my Okonomiyaki cart.
Signed, Ukyo Kuonji
COME TO THINK OF IT...

THE OKONOMIYAKI CART WAS RIPPED OFF BY RAN-CHAN'S *OLD MAN!*
YOU MEAN...
YOU DON'T HAVE IT ANYMORE?
LA LA LA...

...I CAN AT LEAST COLLECT WHAT RANMA LOST TO ME.
WELL... IN ANY CASE...
RUSTLE RUSTLE

HMM... WHAT WAS IT...?
WHAT DID YOU HAVE TO BET?
RANMA?

IT'S BOUND TO BE SOME WORTHLESS LITTLE THING, ISN'T IT?
HA HA HA
I WAS STILL A KID BACK THEN, SO...

FWA
AS WE AGREED...
...I WILL TAKE THE *TENDO DOJO!*
Entitles the Bearer to ownership of the Tendo Dojo.
Signed, Ranma Saotome

KRUKKLE

HEH HEH HEH HEH HEH...
OOOOO WOOOOOO

BUT WHAT *IS* A TENDO DOJO?
A MARTIAL ARTS SCHOOL THAT BELONGS TO MY POP'S FRIEND.

IT'S NOT MINE YET...
BUT SOME-DAY...IT *WILL* BE!

RANMA... YOU ARE SO...
I NEVER SAID ANY-THING OF THE...

SURE YOU DID, RANMA, HONEY!
I REMEMBER HEARING IT MYSELF!
YEEE...
RAAAAN-MAAAA...

I'LL BE BACK TOMORROW TO MOVE IN. PLEASE BE READY TO MORE OUT.
GOOD NIGHT!
HYUUU
いろは
UM...
WELL, IT'S A LEGAL DOCUMENT...
HSST...

...SO YOU GO GET IT *BACK!!!*
K-BOOOM

RANMA...

BOW WOW WOW WOW

BLAST THAT GAMBLING KING...
...WHY DOESN'T HE FIND A NEW HOBBY?
SSS...
SSS...

WHAT'S HE WANT WITH THE DOJO ANYWAY ?!
MUTTER MUTTER
FLIP
NOTHING YOU CAN DO NOW, ANYWAY.

WHY DON'T YOU STAY OVER TONIGHT?
I'LL TAKE GOOD CARE OF YA!
BAP

ST -ST -STAY OVER... T - TONIGHT... ?!
SIZZZZLE
OKONOMIYAKI
UCCHAN'S
OKONOMIYAKI
UCCHAN'S

PART 10
NEVER BET YOUR LIFE

OOOO
BOW WOW WOW
...RANMA ACTUALLY BET THE WHOLE DOJO?
YES. FATHER SEEMS VERY UPSET.
.....
WHAT ARE RANMA AND UKYO THINKING?!
SO JUST STAY HERE TONIGHT.
YOU CAN'T GO HOME, RIGHT?
THANKS, UCCHAN.
ALTHOUGH...WITH THOSE TWO, SOMETIMES IT'S HARD TO TELL...
OKAY, SO THEY'RE CHILDHOOD FRIENDS... BUT THEY'RE STILL A BOY AND GIRL, AFTER ALL...

I WONDER WHAT RANMA IS GOING TO DO?

WHY WOULD HE DO THAT?
MAYBE HE'LL JUST SWITCH OVER TO UKYO NOW.

TRUE. AND SHE'S A COOK...
AND HE DOES LOVE FOOD...
WELL, SHE'S HIS FIANCÉE TOO, RIGHT?

HUH?
AHEM IN ANY CASE, AKANE, HERE'S A CHANGE OF CLOTHES FOR HIM.

.....
WELL, I THOUGHT THAT SINCE RANMA MAY BE STAYING WITH UKYO FOR A WHILE...

RANMA, YOU JERK!
EVERY-THING WAS FINE 'TIL YOU CAME ALONG...
TOLL FREE!
MUTTER MUTTER
CREE CREE CREE

MAYBE HE'LL JUST SWITCH OVER TO UKYO NOW.
HE CAN DO ANYTHING HE WANTS, FOR ALL I CARE.

HYUUUU...
OKONOMIYAKI UCCHAN'S
CLOSED
COME AGAIN!

IT'S OPEN...
HOW CARE-LESS.
KRAA

HEY, RAN--
WHAT'S THERE TO THINK ABOUT, RAN-CHAN?
ORANGES

BE A MAN AND MAKE YOUR CHOICE!
WHICH IS IT GOING TO BE?
BUT I DON'T KNOW WHICH TO GIVE UP.

I'M TIRED OF WAITING...
ERRRGH...
PERK

HE'S...
HE'S CHOOSING WHICH OF US TO MARRY...! HE'S ABOUT TO...
--OKAY! THE ONE I WANT IS RIGHT *HERE!*
AT *LAST*! ♪
WHAT?!
RAN-*MAA*!!
KWAAAA

WHAT'S THE TROUBLE, AKANE?
OH... NOTHING...

"GAMBLING TRAINING"?
YEAH.

YOU JUST WATCH GAMBLING KING. THE DOJO I *LOST* GAMBLING I'LL *WIN BACK* BY GAMBLING!
GNNNNNNG

IF THAT'S WHAT IT'S FOR, I WANT TO HELP.
HA.
JUST DON'T BLAME ME IF YOU GO BANKRUPT.
SSHHFF

IF HE WANTS TO WIN BACK THE DOJO... THEN HE MIGHT WANT...

YAY! I WIN!
ONE MORE TIME!
YAY! I WIN!

ONE MORE TIME!
ONE MORE TIME!

WHY ARE YOU GUYS SO *GOOD?*
YOU'RE KIDDING, RIGHT ... ?
THE QUESTION IS WHY ARE *YOU* SO *BAD?*
sparkle

TARA TARA
B-DUM B-DUM
CASINO KING OPEN

CASINO KING ?
IS IT A NEW ARCADE?
LET'S GO CHECK IT OUT!
TARA
B-DUM B-DUM

CASINO
King
FORMER TENDO DOJO...
HERE IT IS!
BLAH BLAH

OKAY, PLACE YOUR BETS!
YOU LOSE!
K-CHING K-CHING
RED !
BLACK !
OH, NO!
GARRRRRR
C'MON! C'MON!
PART-TIMING.
NABIKI, WHAT ARE YOU DOING?!

IT'S YOUR FUNERAL.
GAMBLING KING! I CHALLENGE YOU TO A MATCH FOR THE OWNERSHIP OF THE TENDO DOJO!
CAR ADVENTURE
EXPLODE!

WHAT WILL YOU GIVE ME IF YOU LOSE?
SO ?

DADDY... !
YOU LOSE.
JOKER

NO LESS...THAN THE TENDO FAMILY'S LIVING ROOM!
VWAAA
Entitles the bearer to ownership of the Tendo Living Room. Signed, Soun Tendo

GAMBLING KING! THIS TIME I CHALLENGE YOU!

HEH HEH HEH!
NOW YOU'LL SEE WHAT *TRAINING* CAN DO!
I WISH I FELT MORE SECURE...
SSHHFF...
I'M COUNTING ON YOU, SON!
Sobb
BAH!
LEAVE IT TO ME.
I BET NO LESS...THAN THE TENDO FAMILY'S FRONT PORCH!
SLAM
Entitles
Beare
Front Porch.
YOU LOSE.
YOU FOOL!
DA-KRROOOM

HOW COULD I LEAVE IT TO THAT TWERP?!
I'LL HAVE TO DO THIS MYSELF!

TENDO KITCHEN !
YOU LOSE.
TENDO HALLWAY!
STAIRS !
Bath room
Tendo dojo
BATH-ROOM !
AKANE'S ROOM !
YOU LOSE.
NABIKI'S ROOM!
HOLD IT RIGHT THERE !

FATHER, IT'S TIME TO STOP.
SHAKE SHAKE
LET'S PLAY !!
FEH...

NO MATTER WHO CHALLENGES ME, IT WILL BE THE SAME.
I'LL TAKE YOU FOR ALL YOU HAVE.
YOU LOSE !
ERK!
JOKER
WOW, NABIKI! YOU DID IT!
SHALL WE GO AGAIN ?

SHE... SHE BEAT ME...
SHE DID WHAT NO ONE ELSE HAS BEEN ABLE TO...
PAST VICTIMS

BUT THEN...SHE *IS* IN HIGH SCHOOL!
GRRRRRR
MAYBE HE CAN'T BEAT ANYONE WHO KNOWS MORE THAN AN ELEMENTARY-SCHOOL STUDENT...
THAT WOULD FIT THE FACTS...

--AND WHAT DOES THAT SAY ABOUT *ME?!*
SHOULD I SPELL IT?
THROW IN RANMA, TOO...

THE LIVING ROOM IS *MINE!*
FWAP
ARRGH!
Entitles Bea
to Tendo
living ro
Soun Tendo

THE ONLY THING LEFT IS THE DOJO!
THIS IS THE LAST STAND...FOR MY *PRIDE!*

LET'S PLAY !!

ONLY ONE THING LEFT TO DO!

WELCOME TO UCCHAN'S!
KRAAAAA
Ucchan's
YEP. SHE'S NOW HERE.
MMM... CUTE WAITRESS !
TEE HEE
Ucchan's

YOU'VE GOT A LOT MORE WORK TO DO TO PAY OFF YOUR LOSSES FROM YOUR "TRAINING."
SHAKKA SHAKKA
IOU one hour work per 1000 yen bet. R. Saotome
GAMBLING... IS MY RUIN...
Sob

PUBLIC BATHS
BLIC BATHS

HMM...
MEANTIME, LET'S KEEP UP THE TRAINING.
COIN LAUNDRY
MONEY at HOME

RAN-CHAN... IS IT POSSIBLE...

...YOU WANT TO GO BACK TO AKANE'S PLACE?
WHA-- ?

OF COURSE NOT !
ANY-HOW...
I CAN'T GO BACK UNTIL I BEAT THAT "KING"!
REALLY ?

I HAVE TO BEAT HIM!
I'M GOING TO STAY HERE UNTIL I *DO!*
GRRR

OH, RANMA !
THAT MEANS YOU'LL LIVE WITH ME *FOREVER!*
SKWEE
MEANING EXACTLY... *WHAT?*
MONTHLY PARKING
SEE ATTENDANT

SUDDENLY I HAVE SO MUCH TIME...
SO MUCH TIME TO WIN RAN-CHAN'S HEART!

WHAT LOSERS.
WHATEVER THE REASON...WE HAVE TO MOVE OUT OF OUR HOUSE.
LIKE I SAID... HE CHEATED!
YOU ONLY HAD TO WIN *ONE* MORE... HOW *COULD* YOU?!
boohoohoo
HEY, *YOU* STARTED THIS MESS, RANMA!
Crowded, ain't it.

COME AND GET ME, PEASANTS!
YEAH...AND *I'M* GONNA *END* IT!

PART 11

PUT ON A POKER FACE

RANMA SAOTOME !
AKANE TENDO !
UKYO KUONJI...
1-F
THEY WERE JUST THERE SLEEPING.
HUH? THEY'RE GONE.
...ARE THEY ALL ABSENT ?
ME TOO !
I'M DONE !
RAN-CHAN... THERE'S NEVER BEEN A PLAYER AS BAD AS YOU.
BUT YOUR FACE-OFF WITH THE KING IS AFTER SCHOOL!
AARGH !

WE CAN'T ALL STAY AT UKYO'S HOUSE FOREVER YOU KNOW...
SHP SHP
YOU'RE WELCOME TO GO...AND LEAVE RAN-CHAN.
I WISH MY WHOLE FAMILY DIDN'T HAVE TO COME...
PRRRRRR
OH, WILL YOU STOP WORRYING?! I'M GONNA WIN BACK YOUR HOUSE AND DOJO!
HOW CAN YOU BE SO POSITIVE?
WANT ME TO TELL YOU HOW TO BEAT HIM...?
NABIKI...?

I'M THE ONLY ONE WHO'S EVER BEATEN HIM, RIGHT?
HE CHEATED, AND BEAT ME AT THE END...
BUT WHILE I WAS PLAYING...
I NOTICED A HABIT THAT THIS "KING" HAS...
A HABIT... !?

YES! FOR EXAMPLE...
SHA

IF YOU PUSH UP THE OLD MAID...
...JUST A LITTLE...
...LIKE THIS, SO IT'S EASY TO GRAB...
JOKER

IS THAT TRUE !?
HE ALWAYS PICKS THAT CARD!
JOKER
JOKER

YOU'VE GOT TO BE KIDDING ME! NOBODY OVER *SIX* WOULD FALL FOR A TRICK LIKE THAT!
PIK

WH- WH- WHAT'S THAT !?

AND THAT'S NOT ALL. HE'S GOT ANOTHER FATAL WEAKNESS!

WHAT WAS THAT... LITTLE RANMA?
ping!

WHEN THE KING IS HOLDING THE OLD MAID...
GLINT

...AND YOU PLACE YOUR HAND ON IT...
...HE STARTS TO LOOK REALLY HAPPY.

SO YOU SWITCH TO A DIFFERENT CARD...
...AND THEN HE LOOKS LIKE THE END OF THE WORLD IS COMING.

OF COURSE... HE'S NOT THE ONLY ONE.
HYUUUUU...
NO WONDER HE CAN'T WIN.

CASINO
King

PWAAAA
K-TAK K-TAK

DADDY'S GOTTEN BETTER, RIGHT?
WELL... HE *SAYS* HE HAS...
I CHALLENGE YOU!
SHA

いろは
SO, YOU'VE COME FOR ANOTHER BEATING, EH, PEASANTS?
WE'VE COME TO RECLAIM OUR HOME...
...AND OUR DOJO!
御守
AKANE, WHERE'S RANMA?
WELL...

I'LL BE THERE...AS SOON AS I GET RID OF THIS WEAKNESS!
JUST DRAG THE MATCH OUT UNTIL THEN.
EASIER SAID THAN DONE...

LET'S PLAY !!
YOU ARE ALL DOOMED.

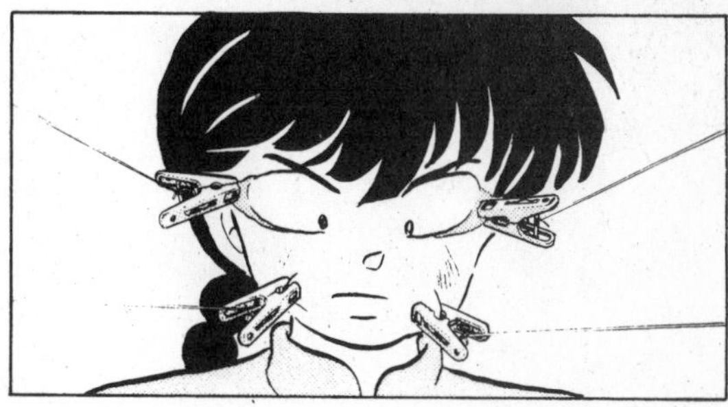

HURRY RANMA...
EVEN IF YOU WON'T DO ANY GOOD...

VMMM

heh
ping

THAT'LL KEEP HAPPENING...AS LONG AS YOU KEEP REACTING.
MOOSH
YOU'RE JUST NOT MADE FOR GAMBLING.
I WON'T GIVE UP!

I CAN'T STOP THIS TRAINING UNTIL I HAVE NO FACIAL EXPRESSIONS AT ALL!

I'M TAKING MY ROOM BACK!
FWA
I WIN!
Entitles Bearer to Nabiki's Bedroom. Signed, Soun Tendo

CASINO King

I'LL TAKE BACK MY ROOM.
AND ME!
AND SO DO I! I'LL TAKE THE KITCHEN.
Entitles Bearer to Akane's room
Entitles Bearer to

THE LIVING ROOM IS MINE!
THE BATH-ROOM IS MINE!
THE PORCH IS MINE!
DAAA-DDY!
ONE MORE GAME!
YOU LOSE.
SHP SHP
THAT'S MY GIRLS!
WELL DONE!

...AND I HAVE THE YARD!
I HAVE THE HALL-WAYS...
I'VE GOT THE STAIRS!
I WIN!
ONE MORE GAME!
CAR ADVENTURE

YES.
I SHOULD START MAKING DINNER SOON.
WELL...THAT'S THE WHOLE HOUSE. SHALL WE GO?
FWAP

SKREEK
I BET THE LIVING ROOM!
THE ONLY THING LEFT IS THE DOJO!
BAM
Entitles Bearer to

ENOUGH IS ENOUGH, FATHER.
DM DM DM DM
EEYAGGA...!
DADDY, IF YOU DO THAT ONE MORE TIME--

WELL, RANMA... YOU NEVER MADE IT...
SO NOW...

AKANE...
DAD! LET ME DO IT!
ZIP
Entitles Bearer to Akane's room. Signed, Soun Tendo

...IT'S ALL UP TO *ME!*
LET'S PLAY!

CAR
STOP !
PLAY

THE VICTORY... WILL BE *MINE.*
SHMM
I'M TAKING OVER.
WE ALMOST MADE IT...
OH, NOOO.

RANMA... LEVEL WITH US...
HAVE YOU ACTUALLY GOTTEN ANY BETTER?
NOT ONE LITTLE, TINY BIT.

NONE ?!
NO MATTER WHAT, THE EXPRESSIONS KEPT COMING.

YES.
BUT THANKS TO THE TRAINING...

...AT LEAST NOW YOU CAN'T *SEE* MY EXPRESSIONS!
ta-DAA

GASP! HE'S RIGHT!
TALK ABOUT PUTTING ON A GAME FACE...!
WHAT A SACRI-FICE...

ALL RIGHT, RANMA SAOTOME!
PAM
BECAUSE OF YOUR DETERMINATION...I AGREE TO A ONE-ON-ONE MATCH WITH YOU.
YOU'VE GOT IT.
HUH...?

...IF HE DIDN'T HAVE A *PLAN* FOR BEATING RANMA!
erk!
HE WOULDN'T BE ACTING SO NOBLE...
I DON'T TRUST THIS GUY!

HERE!
THE DEED TO UCCHAN'S OKONOMIYAKI!
AND WHAT WILL YOU WAGER?
FWAP
Entitles bearer to
WHA...?

UKYO, ARE YOU SURE?!
THAT'S YOUR LIVELIHOOD...
IT DOESN'T MATTER, EITHER WAY.

BECAUSE IN CASE RAN-CHAN LOSES... WE HAVE AN AGREEMENT.
AN... AGREEMENT... ?
BUT... BUT WHAT CAN IT...?

YOU WILL LOSE, RANMA SAOTOME.
HEH! EVEN WITH MY EMOTIONS CONCEALED?
SMIRK
HE IS JUST *NOT* MADE FOR GAMBLING... !
HE'S SMILING !
HE SURE IS!

PART 12
THE VIRTUES OF TRAINING

NOW, IT'S ONE ON ONE...AT *OLD MAID!*
YADA YADA YADA
CASINO
King

I WAGER THE TENDO DOJO !
I WAGER UCCHAN'S OKONOMIYAKI !

IF HE LOSES... HE'LL BECOME YOUR COOK?!
YEP.
HE PROMISED ME.

I'M SO SORRY YOU LOST YOUR BUSINESS BECAUSE OF ME...
HWOOOOOOO
SHUCKS, HONEY...WE PROMISED NOT TO BRING THAT UP AGAIN, REMEMBER?
OKONOMIYAKI
Ucchan's
SHKK SHKK

AND EVENT-UALLY...

SSHHH

YOU'RE...

...YOU'RE SO...
...SO GOOD...
...TO ME...

OH, RANMA...
OH, UCCHAN...
BLUSH

IT'S MEANT TO BE!
OH, RANMA!
OH, UCCHAN!
UM... HELLO...?

IT'S INCREDIBLE!
WHAT A MATCH!

HHHHSSSSSSS
VMM
YADA YADA

C'MON... TAKE THE OLD MAID!
NYU
JOKER

THE JOKER! AGAIN!
YAAGH!
SMIRK

TRY THIS!
NYU
JOKER

HA HA! GOT YOU!
OH, NO!
GASP

THEY'RE PASSING THE JOKER BACK AND FORTH!

YES... YES! THEY'RE BOTH--
THE TWO OF THEM ARE EQUALLY MATCHED!

EQUALLY STUPID !!
HHHHSSSSSSSS

WAIT A SECOND !
THAT'S--
JOKER
2

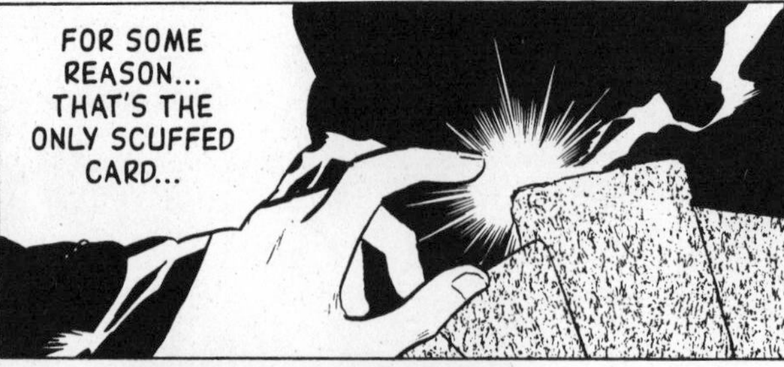
FOR SOME REASON... THAT'S THE ONLY SCUFFED CARD...

BY SLIPPING THE JOKER BACK AND FORTH FOR HOURS...
--I'VE GOT IT!

JOKER
...YOU'RE HOPING TO WEAR ME DOWN!

!
OOOO!!
SHWA!
I'VE SEEN THROUGH YOUR TECHNIQUE!
JOKER

HEH.
GACK!!
JOKER

I WON'T BE TAKING THE JOKER THIS TIME!
HEH HEH HEH...

WHY, THAT -- !
WHILE RANMA WAS BUSY DRAWING A CARD...
...THE KING SLIPPED THE OLD MAID INTO HIS HAND!
HE'S CHEATING !
IS THAT WHAT HAPPENED ?!
FASTER THAN THE EYE COULD FOLLOW!
QUIT IT, AKANE !
BUT... BUT...
COME ON, KING! TAKE A CARD!
FEH.
NYU
JOKER
I COMMEND YOU, RANMA SAOTOME.
GLARE
BUT I WILL NOT GO DOWN EASILY!

KNOW THE FOLLY OF CHALLENGING THE GAMBLING KING!
KWONK

TANG

KSSHH

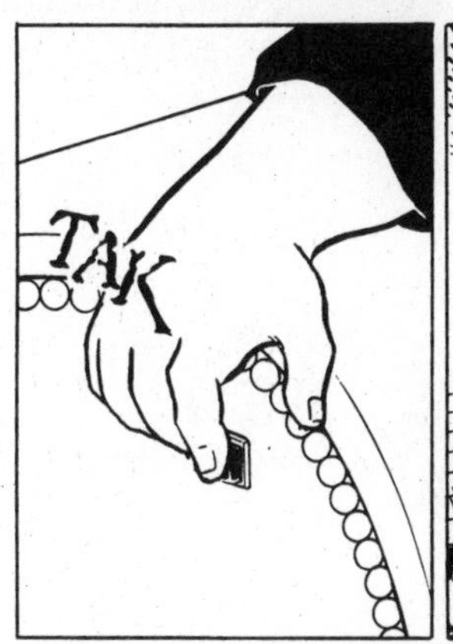
TAK

ZZNGZZNG ZZNG ZZNG

WHY... YOU... LITTLE...
POIK
PING

MOOSH

ALL RIGHT, THEN...
GRRR

PA
PA
OH, YEAH ?!
TAKE THIS! JOKER SHOWER!
FWOOOSHHHH
!
HUH ?!
MNCH
MNCH
GULP

AND THAT'S WHEN RANMA'S AT HIS BEST!
THE GAME'S GETTING OUT OF CONTROL!
AMAZING !
HE ATE ALL THE JOKERS!
OHHH!

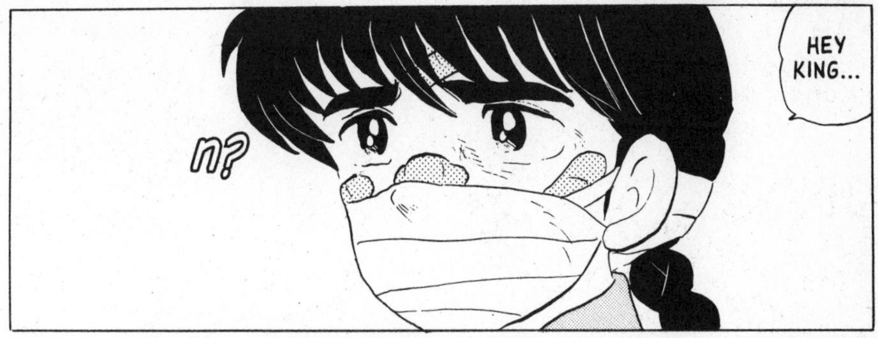
HEY KING...
n?

EH ?

RANMA-HONEY LOOKS SO...SO SAD!
WH-WHAT'S THE MATTER WITH HIM...?
Hit 'im!

ALL I WANTED...
WAS TO PLAY ONE FAIR GAME WITH YOU...

...TO PROVE I COULD BEAT YOU...
GNNG

I TRAINED FOR WEEKS!
B-BUT YOU...
YOU HADDA...
WAAAA!
R- RANMA...
I DIDN'T KNOW HE CARED SO MUCH ABOUT CARDS...
YOU MEAN... I WAS YOUR PERSONAL TEST...?
GAAAAASP
I'M...
SOBB
I'M SORRY, RANMA SAOTOME!
THEN...YOU UNDERSTAND...!
BONK

HERE ARE TWO CARDS.
JOKER
fwa

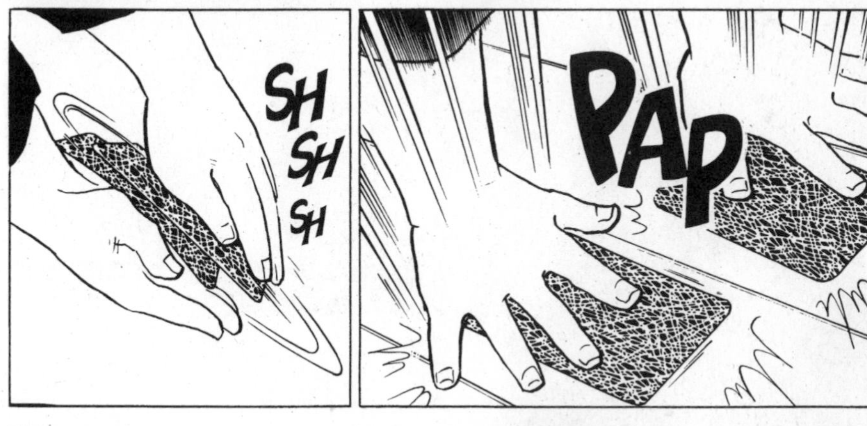
SH SH SH
PAP

FAIR AND SQUARE.
IF YOU PICK THE JOKER, YOU LOSE.
GWI!
OKAY!
GLMP!

HERE GOES !
SHH
SMIRK
CAN IT BE...?
THE KING'S SMILING !
HE MUST HAVE SWITCHED THE CARDS...SO THAT THEY'RE *BOTH* JOKERS!
HE'S CHEATING !
RANMA, DON'T PICK A CARD!
SHWA

HWOOOOOO
TROMP TROMP
RANMA...
SHH-OOH
I WIN.
heh
FWIP
OH... RANMA! SON!
HUH?
SOBB SOBB
CLAP CLAP CLAP CLAP
PING

END OF RANMA 1/2 VOLUME 13.